THE
BATTLE
FOR
ANDY

THE
BATTLE
FOR
ANDY

ANN CORRELL

Tate Publishing & Enterprises

Published by Tate Publishing & Enterprises, LLC
127 E. Trade Center Terrace | Mustang, Oklahoma 73064 USA
1.888.361.9473 | www.tatepublishing.com

Tate Publishing is committed to excellence in the publishing industry. The company reflects the philosophy established by the founders, based on Psalm 68:11,
"The Lord gave the word and great was the company of those who published it."

Book design copyright © 2011 by Tate Publishing, LLC. All rights reserved.
Cover design by Amber Gulilat
Interior design by Chelsea Womble

Published in the United States of America

ISBN: 978-1-61739-521-5
1. Fiction, Christian, General
2. Fiction, Family Life
11.01.13

This book is dedicated to my children, grandchildren, and great-grandchildren. Being a parent gives us the opportunity to teach our children but also lets us learn from them as well.

The credit for this story goes to God. If not for His Word and guidance, it would not have been possible.

Acknowledgments

Thanks to Darrel and Dolores Ilstrup and Irene Olin for their time to edit this work and for the love and encouragement they have given me from the beginning. I also need to say thank you to Janet Staats, who encouraged me to submit this story for publication. There are many dear brothers and sisters who have held me up in prayer, giving me the confidence to continue.

Introduction

God's Word tells us that there are battles we will fight in the world, but we also fight battles within ourselves. Matthew 26:41 tells us to "keep alert and pray. Otherwise temptation will overpower you. For though the spirit is willing enough, the body is weak!" How do we use the Word of God when we find ourselves fighting these battles? The purpose of this book is to help readers discover the value of knowing how to use God's Word to find solutions, comfort, and peace when the world and our own minds seem to turn against us. We are told that the one thing we can all count on is that trial and sorrow will touch our lives.

To some, the Bible is a book of history, to others a novel or biographies of ancient people. There are even those who read the holy text to find errors that may validate their point of view.

The most tragic examples are those who do not read God's Word at all. The word *remember* is used over fifty times in just the first five books of the Bible and over two hundred times throughout Scripture. My point is, how do you remember something you have never heard or read? Jesus first says, "Remember what I've told you," then in John 14:26 tells us that the Holy Spirit will both teach and *remind* us of what he said.

It is for these reasons that I have tried to use God's Word as the source of instruction given to the young boy, Andy. His spirit is growing strong with spiritual food while being protected from an evil that would destroy him if possible.

Although every word in the holy text we call the Bible is for our instruction and the edification of God, I pray I've selected appropriate scriptures throughout the Word to tell the story of man in his quest for knowledge of what life is or should be.

Chapter One

With the first gleam of light, Andy opened his eyes to a day that promised to be full of wonder and surprise. It was his seventeenth birthday. Wiping sleep from his eyes, he remembered what his dad had said the night before. "At twelve, a boy steps on the threshold of manhood, and it is a special time. But with each birthday after that, you will make more and more decisions that will impact the rest of your life." Today was that day for Andy, and he was very anxious to get started. Rushing to get dressed, Andy caught his image in the mirror, with his bright blue eyes and tousled blond wavy hair.

He thought he looked like his father and felt pleased that he would become the image of a man he loved and respected. Andy and his father had worked out an agreement when he turned twelve. When Andy wanted to approach a subject for a man-to-man discussion, he would call his father "Harold." This signaled Harold that Andy would be allowed to voice his opinion without fear of reproach or criticism. Andy also understood that when they were on a level playing field, Harold would also speak his mind without holding back. They each knew that if the subject were one that could cause harm in any way, Harold would invoke a father's privilege to make the final call. Harold was a man of God's word, and during these conversations, he knew that imparting the knowledge of God's Word would sustain Andy throughout his life.

Andy narrowed his eyes in deep thought as he tried to remember how many times Harold had actually had the last word. He had never really taken the time to think about it, but just this moment he realized that his father had always used Scripture to back up his position by saying, "Let's get God's opinion in this talk." Harold had always ended the talks with a gentle suggestion that Andy give more thought to his dad's opinion based on the Word of God.

Andy stopped reflecting on the past and said to the image in the mirror, "Hey, it's your birthday. What are you standing around for?" He was charged with excitement as he ran his fingers through his hair and raced to the head of the stairs. For one fleeting second, he considered sliding down the banister, which was his favorite way to reach the ground floor but always brought a scolding look from his mom when he was caught. He decided against it because of the dignity he now felt he needed to demonstrate. When Andy reached the bottom of the stairs, dignity was forgotten as he started yelling, "Mom…Dad!" Running from one room to another, Andy found only the neatly kept rooms full of familiar furnishings that had made this house his home from the day he came into this world.

Andy saw a note on the fireplace mantle.

This is probably part of the surprise, he thought as he grabbed the note.

Be back soon. Left you some pancakes in the refrigerator.
Love, Mom—P.S. Happy birthday.

A big smile covered his face as he ran to the kitchen and popped all six pancakes into the microwave. As Andy was chewing the last bite of pancake, the doorbell rang. A slightly lopsided smile crossed his face as he started imagining what surprise would be waiting for him on the other side of the door. Maybe the car he and his dad looked at just last week. Andy wanted to be cool and just saunter toward the door and graciously accept the wonderful gift that waited on the other side. It took all of four steps for Andy to lose his composure and race the remaining distance like he was finishing a marathon.

When Andy finally threw the door open, two strangers in dark blue suits stood on the porch. For a split second he couldn't imagine what they had to do with his birthday surprise. The man who rang the bell just stood there looking at Andy. The few silent seconds that passed seemed like a very long time. Beginning to feel uncomfortable, Andy finally said, "May I help you?"

"Are you Andy Staple?" asked one of the men.

"Yes. Why?"

"Are your folks Sarah and Harold Staple?" said the other man, who now stepped closer to the open door. Andy didn't know why, but the last question set off an alarm in his head. He just shook his head and looked from one man to the other, waiting for the next question. Holding up what looked like a thin wallet, the first man said, "I'm Sergeant Brooks, and this is Sergeant Reynolds. May we come in?" Again, Andy just shook his head and stepped back to let the men step into the entryway. The silence was frightening; Andy felt like something had taken most of the air out of the room and it was hard to breathe.

Brooks and Reynolds looked around to see as much of the house as they could from where they stood. Finally, Sergeant Reynolds said, "You here alone?"

"Yes, but Mom and Dad will be back any second." Andy dug the note out of his back pocket and gave it to Sergeant Brooks.

After reading the note, the two men quickly glanced at one another. Sergeant Brooks said, "I'm afraid they won't, Andy. There's been an accident."

Questions flooded Andy's mind so fast he found it impossible to speak. Andy stood perfectly still with his eyes fixed on Sergeant Brooks. Finally, finding his voice that was barely more than a squeak, he asked, "Where are they? What happened? Are they okay?" All this rolled out like one question, giving no time for answers.

Sergeant Reynolds put his hand on Andy's shoulder, gave a gentle squeeze, and said, "Do you have any other relatives close by, Andy?"

"Yeah, kind of...Aunt Margaret lives close, but we don't see very much of her."

"Got a phone number for her?"

Andy just shook his head as he turned toward a small desk that held the phone. Rolling through the Rolodex, Andy found a card, pulled it out, and handed it to Sergeant Reynolds, who had followed him to the phone. Reynolds handed the card to Brooks as he asked Andy if they could sit down somewhere. Andy led Reynolds into the living room and motioned to an overstuffed chair across from the couch. Andy walked to the couch and sat very rigidly on the edge of one of the pillowed seats.

After taking a few deep gulps of air, Andy finally found his voice again and said, "What's going on?"

Before he got an answer, Brooks walked into the living room. "Your Aunt Margaret will be here as soon as she can."

Reynolds pulled on the front of his blue jacket and leaned forward toward Andy to try to answer his question. "Like I said, there was an accident. At the corner of Fourth and Vine, a car ran a stop sign, and your mom and dad had just pulled out into the intersection."

Andy almost whispered, "Are Mom and Dad okay?"

Brooks walked over to the couch and stood behind Andy. His posture was very straight and professional, but there was a cloud of sadness in his eyes and sympathy in his voice as he quietly answered, "I'm afraid not, son."

• •

Matt and Margaret Selby were successful in their marriage of twenty-seven years and their professional lives. Two years earlier, Matt enjoyed seeing his name printed on the door of a respected brokerage firm, and Margaret was an attorney with the Tory and Banson law firm. They spent time together at the gym and enjoyed competing with the loser having to buy a fruit drink at the health bar. Matt enjoyed handball and golf, and Margaret spent a lot of time, money, and effort keeping her blonde hair blonde and maintaining her perfect size nine.

Matt left for work, and Margaret was enjoying her second cup of coffee when the phone rang. *Who on earth could be calling this early?*

"Hello, Margaret Selby speaking."

"Mrs. Selby, this is Sergeant Brooks. I'm afraid I have some bad news."

"Did something happen to Matt?"

"This is about your brother, Harold, and his wife, Sarah. They were both killed in a car accident this morning. Your nephew said you were the closest relative here, and he is going to need your help."

"I'll be there as soon as possible." Margaret's answer was automatic, as she was numbed by the news she had just heard.

She sat down at the kitchen table, where she had left her cup of coffee, and stared into the black liquid as she tried to sort out her feelings and next step. Tears trickled down her face as memory took her back to the farm where she and Harold played chase and swung on a tire swing. Those were happy days for Margaret, and she lingered in the past for a few minutes. Slowly, the reality of the news took hold.

Margaret thought about her feelings toward Harold. While they had remained civil, they had very little interaction, as their lives had moved in different directions. As her mind slowly moved toward the present, she thought about when she lived with Harold and Sarah after she graduated from college. He had always been a good brother, always there for her when she needed him. It was during this time that she saw how much Harold had turned to his Christian faith. He didn't really say much about Christ, but his lifestyle screamed Christianity. For some reason she saw this as a holier-than-thou attitude, and it put her on edge. Although it never happened, she was always afraid of having the Bible crammed down her throat. She remembered how happy she was the day she had found a job and moved into a small apartment in town. She didn't like the fact that her attitude was pulling her away from her brother, but she began finding excuses to have something important to do when Harold asked her to spend time with him and his family. This had caused a rift that she hadn't wanted to close.

Composing herself, Margaret thought, *So what's my next step?* Her successful law practice had given her the ability to look at every situation with professional precision and logic. The next step was a phone call to her father, Andrew, and this was a task she dreaded. While Harold used lifestyle as an example, it seemed that Andrew couldn't open his mouth without quoting Scripture. Steeling herself against emotion, Margaret reached for the phone and dialed the seldom-used but never-forgotten number of the family farm on the outskirts of Portland, Oregon. Margaret found herself hoping that Andrew was out and she could just leave a message on the answering machine, but she immediately chastised herself with, "And what would you say, Margaret? 'Harold and Sarah are dead…come ASAP'?"

On the second ring, Margaret heard the familiar voice of Andrew. "Hello!"

"Dad, this is Margaret."

"Hi, Maggie. How are you? Is everything okay?"

"No. There has been an accident. The police just called and said Harold and Sarah were killed in a car wreck."

The silence on the other end of the phone caused Margaret to think about the coldness of how she had just told her father that his only son had just died. She felt a stab of guilt, but her pride would never let her recant.

"Dad, are you still there?"

"Yes, Margaret. I'm here. I'll get the next flight out."

As Margaret hung up the phone, she wondered why her father had sounded so calm. She knew his strength came from his faith in God, but she believed it was a false hope that would someday prove to be a great disappointment.

She remembered her mom dragging her and Harold off to Sunday school and church every Sunday while Andrew got to stay home to take care of chores that always seemed so pressing on Sunday mornings. Andrew was her world when she was young, and she resented the fact that she had to go somewhere he didn't.

Chapter Two

Margaret pulled into the driveway and saw the door standing open. Instead of rushing into the house, she briefly paused on the porch and wondered if she was equipped to deal with the trauma she knew was waiting for her. Thoughts of self-pity changed her initial panic into an emotion that bordered on anger. She thought about how Harold seemed to be a friend to everyone he met and his ability to appear happy, no matter what happened. He enjoyed a peace she never quite understood but that didn't help him now, did it? *Look what it got him! Dead—that's what. Where is his God now? What will Dad and Andy expect of me?* She tightened the grip on her emotions and in little more than a whisper breathed, "Just get this done, Margaret." Squaring her shoulders, Margaret all but marched into the living room.

Reality hit her like a punch to the stomach as she saw one man sitting in her sister-in-law's favorite chair, watching Andy very closely. He seemed to be contemplating something, with two fingers over his mouth and his thumb positioned as if to support his chin. The other was standing behind Andy with one hand lying on Andy's shoulder. Margaret didn't want to look directly at Andy but knew it was inevitable. Her eyes slowly descended to Andy's face, and a feeling as close to pity or possibly guilt as she was able to muster grabbed her heart.

Still, she didn't rush to the side of her nephew, who sat very still, staring at something that only he could see and looking much younger than she expected. "What exactly happened?" she demanded.

"As I told you on the phone, ma'am, an older couple ran the stop sign going east where Fourth crosses Vine Street. Your brother and his wife had just pulled into the intersection and were hit broadside by the other car doing about forty miles an hour."

"Where are the people who were driving the other car?" Margaret said through clenched teeth. "Don't worry, Andy; I'll see to it that they are prosecuted to the full extent of the law." Only when there was no response from Andy did she realize how bad her timing was with such a statement. Sergeants Brooks's and Reynolds's looks reinforced her realization. Margaret could feel the flush rising in her cheeks as she slowly walked toward Andy. Kneeling down in front of the boy, she gently put her hand on his knee. "Don't worry, honey. Your Grandfather Staple will be here soon."

"Could we talk privately for a few minutes, Mrs.…?" Sergeant Reynolds was looking directly into Margaret's eyes with his head slightly tipped, waiting for an answer to his unfinished question.

"Uh, Selby, Sergeant. Margaret Selby. I was Harold's older sister. Let's go into the kitchen. I could use a cup of coffee."

"Good idea." Reynolds gave a quick look at Andy then followed her into the kitchen.

"What now, Sergeant?" The question was more in Margaret's eyes than her voice.

"We will take care of the accident report, but the situation here with the boy is in your hands. Will that be a problem, Mrs. Selby?"

Margaret reflected back to when there had been some warmth between her and her brother. After her marriage to Matt, their lives slowly moved toward those who could promote their careers, and that certainly did not include her brother, who owned and operated a successful but modest-sized auto repair shop.

Hearing her name, she returned her attention to the question Sergeant Reynolds had asked, answering, "Harold and Sarah did have a will. There's a copy in my office. It was Harold's wish that if something happened to him and Sarah, Andy would go live with our father. That's why I called him before I came over here. He lives in Portland, so he could be here within the hour if he can get a flight." Margaret was still a little reflective, but her answer was that of a lawyer, not an aunt, sister, or even daughter.

⁂

When Andrew Staple answered the call from Margaret, his sorrow was intensified by the coldness in Margaret's voice. He not only felt the pain of grief for the loss of a son but deep remorse for the loss of his daughter. *My Lord and my God, what can I do? Am I really capable of raising another family now? And how can I help Maggie find her way back to your throne?* He remembered the scripture, "She obeys no one, she accepts no correction. She does not trust in the Lord, she does not draw near to her God" (Zephaniah 3:2). He quoted the scripture like a question.

Keeping silent before his God, Andrew turned to God's Word for strength. He would remind the Lord of what he promised and hold the truth of it without compromise. *You said that when I couldn't understand why something happened, I should trust in you with all my heart. This is one of those times, Lord, because I don't understand why you would allow this to happen now.* As he continued to dwell in God's Word, he felt the peace that surpassed his understanding slowly take hold of his mind. God's Word raced through his mind so quickly he hardly had time to digest one point of grace before another began.

With tears of relief, all Andrew could say was, "Thank you, Lord. Thank you. I always find peace and strength in your Word." The Holy Spirit reminded Andrew of the words, *Let the morning bring me word of your unfailing love, for I have put my trust in you. Show me the way I should go, for to you I lift up my soul.*

With tears of sorrow, Andrew knelt before the Lord, knowing that his spirit would receive the calming comfort given by the Holy Spirit. Andrew's spirit became very still and quiet. Then, in what sounded like a shout in his mind, he heard, *Get to Andy as fast as possible. There is a spiritual battle to be fought, and he needs your help.*

· ·

It was fortunate that there were several flights a day between Portland and Pasco, Washington. By ten o'clock that morning, Andrew was boarding a plane for Pasco and his grandson. They were small commuter planes, but other than the first flight in the morning and one at the end of the workday, there were always seats available. As soon as Andrew found his seat, stowed his one piece of luggage, and buckled up, he closed his eyes to speak to the only person he knew with the wisdom to lead his actions and control the situation.

Lord, I need your reassurance. When I agreed to take Andy, there was the confidence that it would never be necessary. Parents expect their children to outlive them. You know I will bow to your plan and accept that your reason for putting Andy in my care is not for me to know until the appointed time, but I can't help but think about my own children. Margaret and Harold are examples of mankind. One chose the light, and the other chose darkness.

Andrew drifted back to a time before his rebirth, when God had not influenced his life. It was a critical time, when events and attitudes influenced his children's lives. Knowing that he was the main player in these memories, Satan still planted doubt in Andrew's mind about God's forgiveness for the past. These doubts always began a battle of resistance and reaffirmation that the person responsible for those sins no longer lived.

He could still see his wife Nan bustling around the kitchen of the old farmhouse. Nan spent most of her time in her kitchen. It was a sunny room and a happy place most of the time. You could always smell something baking or see a towel thrown over a delightful surprise that you knew would bring a playful slap if you tried to peek. People very seldom went into the living room because hospitality began and flourished at the big, oak kitchen table. Andrew smiled when he remembered those times. It was those little things that made a family unique and planted wonderful flowers in your secret memory garden.

Andrew smiled when he remembered his darling little Maggie wobbling from one chair to the next and looking at him for the praise she felt she deserved when she made it to the next chair. He knew he was Maggie's world, and so did Nan.

He could still hear Nan ask, "Will you just think about going to church with us tomorrow, Andrew? You know how much it would please all of us. Every Sunday Maggie cries to stay home with you."

And he always answered, "We'll see. You know there is always a lot to do around here."

"If you would let the Lord help you with the farm, things would go a lot smoother," Nan would answer.

"The Lord isn't going to plow the ground or plant the seed."

"I know. But he can help in ways we can't even imagine if you'd just give him a chance."

Lord, why was I so stubborn, so self-centered? All I could see was how hard I had to work. Never once did I stop to notice that Nan was always up before me and still cleaning long after I had gone to bed, making sure that whatever I needed was ready before I even asked. And her humming, always humming…always satisfied even when circumstances were hard. Why didn't I realize she worked as hard as I did? In my sin, I remember thinking that if she had worked as hard as I had, she wouldn't have the energy to hum.

As the years passed, I realized that Maggie was taking all this in. Year after year, she drifted more toward my attitude. I realized the harm I'd caused the day Maggie told her mother that she had decided if I didn't need the church then neither did she. I'll never forget the look in Nan's eyes—no judgment or condemnation in that look, just sadness and pity. As I turned to leave the room with Maggie trailing behind me, I knew in my heart that one small spark in Nan died that day.

I know you have forgiven my past sins and put them as far from you as the east is from the west, but the knife of guilt still pierces my heart. I loved my children equally, and my chastisement was fair and given with love and concern, and yet… Andrew paused with a sigh that originated from the very bottom of his soul. *The seed had already been planted with Maggie.*

He wasn't sure how to pray about the many questions running through his mind. For the past thirty years, Andrew had presented life's problems to the Lord, both large and small. At times like this, he would picture himself standing before the throne of God, praising the worthiness of the Lamb, allowing his mind to repeat the promises in the Word that God would answer his petition. Then, quieting his mind, he waited for instruction.

Peace and a sense of well-being always surrounded Andrew when he waited on the Lord to tell him what to do. Andrew was more than a little perplexed when his spirit heard a question instead of an answer. *What do you want from me?* He sat there for a long time considering the question and how to answer, even though it seemed like the answer should be obvious.

I need you to tell me what to do about Andy. I need your words of wisdom so I don't fail. With this, Andrew again approached the throne, but this time he saw himself on his knees and very humble.

The answer was so loud and clear in his mind that Andrew could not believe the man sitting next to him on the plane didn't hear the response. *You already have my Word. Haven't I told you to "ask and it will be given to you; seek and you will find; knock and the door will be opened to you"?*

"For everyone who asks, receives; he who seeks, finds; and to him who knocks, the door will be opened" (Matthew 7:7–8). Search, seek, and study, and you will have the answers to all your questions."

Andrew returned to reality just as the plane touched down at the Pasco airport. The man sitting next to him asked, "Did you enjoy your rest?"

"Yes, thank you. It was very refreshing and enlightening."

Andrew had reserved a car and in a very short time was headed for the parking lot. He stopped when he saw a pay phone and decided to call ahead to let them know he was there.

"Staple residence."

"Is that you, Maggie?"

"Oh, yes, Dad. Where are you?"

"I'm here. I've rented a car and will be there in about fifteen minutes unless you need me to stop for something."

Margaret waited too long to answer and Andrew knew that she was trying to find a way to avoid their inevitable meeting.

"Maggie, you still there?"

"Oh, yes…sorry. Actually, I would really appreciate it if you could come right to the house. I have an appointment I couldn't get out of, and I'm already late."

Andrew knew this was Margaret's escape speech and that she would be gone by the time he arrived at his son's home.

He grabbed his bag and set out to find the mid-sized car he had rented. Sitting behind the wheel, he suddenly found himself needing to talk things over with the Lord again. *Father, this is going to be so difficult. Please give me strength to get through this, and help me keep my attention focused on Andy and my faith in you. If there is any way for me to witness to Maggie and Matt, open the door. But I will follow your lead.* Even though his heart felt as if someone had filled it with lead, his mind and body were revived and refreshed as he started the car.

Chapter Three

Hearing the call from the throne of God excited Nahal, Darak, and Lanchotaam. A feeling of anticipation was overshadowed only by the thought of the responsibility that would soon be theirs to carry.

Even mighty warriors of heaven approached the Light with fear and trembling. They knew that once they entered the Light, an overpowering love would replace the fear of uncertainty with strength and determination to complete the assignment they would be given. Approaching the first level, they entered a thin, white mist, which filled them with reverence and excitement. This was the level of decision and the easiest for mankind to pass through once the soul decided to take the first step of faith. They knew people felt this first step was safe. Stepping into the mist, they immediately began a climb. They knew the journey would become more difficult as they ascended toward the Master.

With the mist of the first level behind them, a clear, beautiful valley lay before them. This was the valley of determination and, for some, uncertainty about commitment. Beyond the valley was a thick cloud so dense one could lose their way if not for the grace and guidance they knew would be provided. All who passed through the valley felt a sense of well-being. The air was fresh; each breath revitalized the soul as an icy tinkle surged through every molecule of one's being.

There was a feeling of satisfaction that a soul felt for making the decision to accept God's gift of salvation. However, there were some that didn't have the will to enter into the unknown of walking by faith and not sight. They knew great reward was given to those who continued the journey to a higher plateau and deepening of the spirit.

Lanchotaam, Darak, and Nahal swiftly passed through the valley and entered the third level of their destination. One step into the dense fog produced a feeling of humility but also a hunger for wisdom. The path soon became very narrow and could only be felt, not seen. They had to climb by faith. Having made this trip many times throughout history, they knew the secret was keeping their eyes on the throne. At the beginning of their journey, the throne was a faint, golden glow. Their spirits were focused on the promises God gave his children; they were always flooded with an indescribable feeling of peace and joy as they looked forward to any service they could give his heirs. Climbing ever higher, they took comfort in the knowledge that the glow would become brighter as they approached their objective. Even though the time required for angels to pass through the third level was relatively short, they knew that, to mankind, it would take a lifetime.

As the glow became as large as the universe, it surrounded Lanchotaam, Darak, and Nahal with bolts of white lightning and thunder so deafening the human instinct would be to flee if he or she had the ability to move. They knew that they were entering the presence of Almighty God.

Lanchotaam, Darak, and Nahal immediately fell prostrate at the edge of the glow and waited to be given their assignment. There was no audible sound, but each knew why they were created. Lanchotaam was an angel created to protect the spirit when the soul is determined to seek God and his will. Darak, an angel of the flesh, was created to walk hand in hand with men. And Nahal was an angel created to protect, sustain, and gently guide the soul. These were not guardian angels; Lachotaam, Darak, and Nahal were warriors created to enter into spiritual battle.

A voice with the force of a great storm yet as gentle as the voice of a mother reassuring her small child filled their awareness. "The lion stalks a new prey. I have chosen warriors created to protect the soul, spirit, and flesh of the young boy, Andy. This lamb is mine, and I will not have him tempted beyond what he can bear. Nahal, the beginning of this assignment will be more difficult for you than the others, for the soul is the catalyst that determines action of the flesh and attitude of the mind. You will see that the soul is sustained and understands my grace until there is sufficient growth in understanding to continue the path toward wisdom. Darak, when the enemy knows the target of my attention, he will double his efforts to influence this soul to look at material benefits rather than spiritual. Much has happened to this youth, and much more will happen that could cause reactions in the flesh fed by anger and bitterness. Protect him against the forces these emotions will summon. Lanchotaam, Andy's spirit will cry out to me in great sorrow. Feed his spirit with the truth that I will always rescue him. The mind and soul in a human always determine growth or destruction for the body and the spirit. You, Lanchotaam, will see the plate of evil and darkness the enemy will try to spoon-feed this boy. Prevent it if Andy allows. Minimize it if he is not aware he has invited the attention of evil."

• • • • • • • • • • • • • • • • • • • •

Satan was alert to the special attention and activity surrounding Andy Staple.

Haphak rushed to answer his summons. The path to his master's throne was easy, well lit, and downhill all the way. Haphak's job was to distort events that would influence a soul to turn toward good. He was very strong and had won many victories.

Haphak always became cynical as he passed through the different stages of hell. His eyes swiftly passed over the souls who chose to believe that the promises of Jesus were fables and obeyed the lord of the world. Each soul in this entry stage desperately clung to whatever gave them a sense of security or belonging. The surroundings were beautiful and offered every kind of pleasure the mind could conceive. Laughter was constant and so loud that it almost rose to the level of hysteria. Drugs, alcohol, and every pleasure of the flesh were easily accessible. Lies, covetousness, hate, and avarice dripped from the walls like honey and became sweeter each time the will of man engaged in another step toward the second death.

As in the heavenly counterpart, one could choose to remain at this entry level. But as time passed, the temptation to see beyond the next door and the promise of a new level of awareness became harder to resist. At first, fear of the unknown stopped some from going further into the teachings of the lord of this place. But with time, their fears abated. A golden door at the end of a corridor was a constant reminder of rewards for those whose will demanded a deeper walk with Satan. No one who chose to go deeper ever returned, but there were rumors about the rewards on the other side. Everyone was sure that there would be total fulfillment and gold was abundant for those that took the plunge. It was never a secret that the master wanted each of them to choose to walk closer to him and his precepts and that he made going deeper very appealing. It was so easy; all you had to do was say yes. It felt as if there was a whisper like a gentle breeze in this first level, quietly promising wealth, honor, position, and power for those who made the commitment.

Another still, small voice was also present at this entry level. The message was one that Haphak knew was the source of many fits of anger for his lord. When Satan allowed himself to think that his sheep could be tempted to turn their backs on all he offered, his anger shook the very foundation of hell, his thoughts weaving the same web since his creation. "Return to the place of your salvation!" he roared. "How dare he influence the wills of those who chose me! Didn't he give me the world as my kingdom?"

As Haphak quickly passed through the golden door, he enjoyed the feeling of self-importance surrounding occupants of this stage. It was a common sight to see one soul who noticed the possession of another engage in any activity necessary to increase his or her own wealth by decreasing the property of the other person. In truth, such activity was rewarded. Even with all their needs met, the most notable emotion that filled the air was greed and selfishness. Nothing was ever enough to satisfy the ravenous appetites these souls possessed. Haphak smiled as he took note of how many souls he was responsible for helping in the decision to follow his true lord. Thoughts of his own reward momentarily saturated his mind but quickly diminished when he thought of the thousands that still resisted the offerings of his master.

The last door was a brilliant, perfect ruby. The glow reflected the brilliance of light and life offered on the other side. Haphak passed through this stage quickly and unnoticed. He too understood that for one to earn the right to pass through the last and final door, a lifetime of obedience to his master was required. He also knew that once a soul passed into the final stage, their reward was indeed well earned.

Haphak prepared himself for his audience. He was never quite sure what experience waited for him as he came face-to-face with Satan. There had been times when victory had given him a sense of confidence and a bittersweet satisfaction that he had, in some way, pleased his master. Defeat was another matter, and Satan was aware of failure simultaneously with the event. Neither was the issue here. Haphak only knew he had been called.

Satan was quiet and reflective, pacing around the room like a caged animal. Haphak knew better than to announce his arrival and was very sure Satan was aware of his presence. Haphak stood quietly for what seemed an eternity until Satan suddenly stopped, spun around to face him, and said, "Andy! Quickly assess the situation and report. I want this soul." With a wave of his hand, Haphak left, and Satan began pacing once again.

It took seconds, as we measure time, for Haphak to reach his destination. Margaret had just arrived, and Haphak took the opportunity to influence her attitude just before she entered the house. His smirk confirmed his assurance that he had the upper hand. As he prepared to return with a positive report to his master, he saw Lanchotaam, Darak, and Nahal hovering over the boy. Knowing he could not delay long, he watched just long enough to be sure they saw the person in charge make her appearance. Lanchotaam's and Haphak's eyes met in a way that left no doubt that each would battle for this boy. Haphak saw their expression as they became aware of the condition of Margaret's heart, and as he swiftly departed, Haphak yelled, "Why waste your time here?" As soon as he left, the three angels looked at each other with knowing smiles.

Haphak was certain his news would please his master, Satan. He had just arrived and was again waiting to be recognized. "Well! Don't just stand there. What is it that's so important about this boy?"

Haphak was taken aback by the sudden recognition. *You would think by now I'd be used to it,* he thought as he opened his mouth to give Satan the good news. "Everything is under control, master. The boy is in a stupor, and the one in control hovers just outside your entry level…Margaret Selby. Margaret Selby is his aunt." Haphak stated this last bit of information like it was the punch line to a joke.

"Excellent," replied Satan, relaxing slightly for the first time since he became aware of the attention God was giving this boy. "This woman and her husband have fallen to one of the greatest sins of this era—greed. You know the demons to send, and your assignment is to oversee the project. There is something special about Andy, and whatever the future holds for him, I want to be the one directing his path. Now go."

Chapter Four

When Andrew arrived, he noticed that Margaret's car was gone. He almost laughed, thinking that her escape had to have been so fast that she probably hadn't taken the time to hang up the phone and he would find it dangling by the cord. As he pulled into the driveway, he whispered to his constant companion, "Here we go, Lord."

When Andrew entered the house, Lanchotaam, Darak, and Nahal saw the Lord living in and walking with Andrew. Each, in turn, bowed in reverence to the Spirit of the Living God so evident in this life. They also shared a smile among themselves, realizing that Haphak left to make his report before he had all the facts. They knew Haphak left with the understanding that Margaret Selby would be in charge of Andy and gave that report to Satan.

Andrew walked into the living room and, putting his finger to his lips, signaled to Reynolds and Brooks to remain silent.

Andy felt relief; disbelief was still present, but something had changed. Climbing out of his stupor was slow and painful, but he sensed a source of warmth and light that was very calming enter the room. Andy suddenly felt a security that had been absent since the doorbell rang early that morning. He looked up and saw his grandfather standing about four feet away with outstretched arms ready to wrap around Andy in a secure love. Without knowing how he accomplished the distance, he fell into the strong, secure, loving arms of his papa. Andy felt safe.

Looking at the detectives over Andy's head, he asked, "Is there anything more you need right now?"

"No. I think we've got everything we need for the moment. Will you be around for a while?"

"That's up to Andy. I'll be here as long as it takes."

The world blurred through tears as Andrew and Andy made their way back to the couch and sat down without breaking the physical or spiritual bond they shared. Andy's heart broke, and the long, painful healing process began with the flood of tears. Andrew held tight, kept quiet, and prayed, *Father, as you give good gifts to your children, bless me now with the wisdom to give Andy what he needs.* As his prayer left the lips of his spirit, Andrew heard himself say, "Let's pray."

"Oh, Papa, I can't pray. What would I say? Right now I think I'm mad at God for letting Mom and Dad die."

"I know. That's why it's so important for you to pray. You see, God wants you to tell him with your mouth what's in your heart." Andrew knew how God's grace healed the anguished heart. "Of course, he already knows what you feel, and he will heal the hurt. But don't make the mistake of shutting him out when you need him most. Trust him, Andy; he really does understand what you are going through. Remember, he lost one very dear to him to a cross. You are thinking that your mom and dad didn't deserve to die so young and leave you alone. God is saying, 'Yes, I know. My Son didn't deserve to die either, but he obeyed the will of his Father.'"

Andy fell to the floor in front of the couch and laid his head on his papa's knee. He began soft and slowly, "Dear God, my mom and dad are gone, and I don't know why. I hurt so bad inside and don't know what to do with the hurt, so could you just make it go away, please?" Andy fell silent for a minute. It felt like someone had taken a hot poker and hit his mind. The next moment, his red-rimmed eyes looked up at the ceiling, and Andrew heard his grandson scream, "No, God. I'm not just hurt; I'm mad! Why did you take my dad and mom?" Andy stopped and seemed to be waiting for an answer as they both sat quietly listening to the grandfather clock's *tic, tic, tic.*

Margaret had come to the entrance of the living room in time to hear Andy's outburst of anger. She didn't make her presence known but thought to herself, *Maybe there's hope for Andy yet. At least he knows enough to blame God for the hurt and pain of death.* Margaret was almost surprised when she felt as if there was a conversation between two people in her mind discussing this topic. *That's right. What kind of a God would take a mother and father on their son's birthday?* She had forgotten it was Andy's birthday until this moment and vowed to do something special to help Andy celebrate.

Andy and Andrew felt a new presence in the room. Looking toward the door, they saw Margaret standing in the entry.

Gently detaching himself from Andy, Andrew stood up and walked toward his daughter with outstretched arms. Margaret dreaded this moment but met her father's embrace with the expected firmness of a dutiful daughter. "How are you, Dad?"

"Not doing to good right at the moment, Maggie…er, I mean Margaret."

"What can I do to help?"

"Since you have all the legal papers, will you make the arrangements for Andy? I would do it, but I really think I need to give Andy all my time and attention right now."

"Sure. Matt and I sort of figured we would be the ones to take care of the burial arrangements, so we left instructions for the hospital to transfer the bodies to the mortuary on Court Street. You and Andy can see them after four tomorrow."

Andy couldn't believe what he was hearing. He stood up and, looking straight into his aunt Margaret's eyes, said in a steady voice,

"It's too bad you didn't love my mom and dad. They were really great people, and they never stopped loving you and Matt." With that, Andy ran through the kitchen and out the back door.

"What was that all about? What got into him?"

"He's very hurt, and you sounded so cold and matter-of-fact about burying his folks."

"Well, that's too bad." Margaret was irritated, and it was evident in her tone. "I don't mind making the arrangements, but there are some things Andy will need to know, and he might as well start growing up and accepting the facts of life right now."

Margaret started toward the back door to find Andy when a voice as strong and firm as thunder stopped her in her tracks. "Stop right there, Margaret!" Margaret felt like she was a small child who had been caught doing something bad and was about to be punished. Needless to say, she didn't like the feeling; after all, she was an adult. When she turned around and faced her father with an attitude ready to battle, she realized she couldn't say one word as her eyes met her father's narrowed eyes. Anger flared up in her mind as she thought, *Why is this happening? I thought I had gotten past this. What can he do anyway?* But still, she could not verbally confront her father.

"Try to exercise a little compassion for Andy's feelings," Andrew said with a softening tone. "If nothing else, try to remember how you felt when you found out Momma had died."

Margaret felt like she had been slapped in the face. Memories of heartbreaking pain seared through her brain as she thought back to what she now considered her black day of freedom from the Christian influence her mother constantly held before her. It was the day she had vowed that a God that would allow her mother to die after loving and serving him all her life didn't deserve her love. *That's right,* came a whisper to her mind.

Haphak did not like some of the emotions Margaret was feeling. He knew it was a critical moment of decision for Margaret, and he wasn't about to let her slip into a mind-set of forgiveness. The helpers he had commissioned were standing close at hand, eagerly waiting for his summon. "Deceit, I want you to remind this mortal who it was that made her miserable every Sunday."

Deceit quickly positioned himself behind Margaret and flooded her mind with the Sundays that she begged to stay home with her father. Did he stick up for her? No! He told her to mind her mother. Even the day she had stood up for herself and refused to go was a bitter victory. She had felt miserable, and if it wasn't his fault, whose was it?

Lanchotaam quickly moved to position himself between Margaret and Deceit. "Remember the morning your mother died? The guilt you felt that in some way her death was your fault? You went to your father and asked him why God had taken your mother, and he said it was because she had done what God had sent her to do, so he allowed her to come home. You thought, *Did she do what God asked her to do, or did she just try and fail because of me? Did my rebellion bring her death?* "No! Mother didn't fail God," Dad had said as gently as possible. "He hasn't failed you or me either, my little Maggie. Death is between the dying flesh and God; no one else is included in that decision."

Lanchotaam sensed an atmosphere of great danger. He immediately called a band of warriors who always stood ready. They instantly surrounded the house, Margaret, and Andrew. Lanchotaam shouted, "Find Andy; protect and comfort him." No less than ten warriors, armed and ready for battle, dispatched toward the backyard. They immediately saw the danger Lanchotaam had sensed.

Andy was sitting in the swing he and his dad had built when he was little more than three years old. Surrounding him were a dozen demons ready to strike with temptation the moment Andy gave them an opportunity. They were very accomplished at their jobs, throwing words like *fault, hate, blame, unfair, hurt,* and *uncaring* at Andy to confuse and keep him off balance. With each word, they diligently watched for one flicker of attitude they could use to begin thoughts of rebellion, disappointment, and eventually hate.

The demonic forces were so busy with Andy that they were not aware of the angelic warriors slowly advancing with swords drawn. By the time the demons sensed an unwanted presence, it was too late. They had seen what the sword of God's warriors had done to other demons. With raised swords they quoted in unison, "Give us aid against the enemy, for the help of man is worthless. With God we will gain the victory, and he will trample down our enemies" (Psalm 60:11–12). These warriors used the same sword the Holy One used on their master two centuries ago.

When the sword of God strikes a demon, the demon is bound.

A heaviness that had been crushing Andy was lifted, his mind returned to the swing and the hours he and his dad had talked about God's Word. A scripture he and Harold had talked about just last week popped into his mind.

> Be self-controlled and alert. Your enemy the devil prowls around like a roaring lion looking for someone to devour. Resist him, standing firm in the faith, because you know that your brothers throughout the world are undergoing the same kind of sufferings. And the God of all grace, who called you to his eternal glory in Christ, after you have suffered a little while, will himself restore you and make you strong, firm and steadfast.
>
> 1 Peter 5:8–10

"I'm yours, God. Guess I always have been. Help me deal with this so you can start teaching me."

Andy remembered the words in Hebrews that reassured him that God is aware of everything that touches His children. After all, nothing in all creation is hidden from His sight. He also remembered that these verses said that God knows the true intent of every deed, and there will be an accounting. He is the great high priest and can understand and sympathize with everything that touches you.

The gentle voice of Andrew broke the quiet. "Why are you smiling, Andy?"

"Because I know that everything is going to work out, Papa. It's going to be fine 'cause God knows how I feel and he is in control."

Margaret had just stepped out the back door and couldn't believe her eyes. Her dad and Andy looked like they were having a good time. *This proves it. There is no logic or common sense to explain how a Christian thinks.* She was irritated when she recalled a confrontation she had with Andrew a while back when he said, "Are you so foolish? After beginning with the Spirit, are you now trying to attain your goal by human effort?"

You will fail, Margaret. The Creator chooses the foolish things of the world to shame the wise. So are you foolish or wise? Margaret remembered a scripture she had read or heard that said something like that but knew it was meant for other situations. She was wise and would prove it very soon.

Chapter Five

Margaret's weak invitation to buy dinner later was declined. "Well, I have some loose ends that need my attention anyway, so this will give me time to clear my schedule. Do you want us to come back tonight, or will you two be okay?"

"We'll be just fine, Maggie. We'll see you tomorrow."

Almost instinctively, Margaret turned to give Andy a hug before she left but felt as if someone grabbed her arm and held her back. *Don't get attached now, girl. It will be twice as hard later, and besides, why be a hypocrite?*

Andy knew by the look on his aunt's face that she was fighting a battle. He reached up and gently cupped Margaret's face in his hands. "It's all right, Aunt Margaret. I understand this is a hard time for you too. You know Papa and I will be praying for you."

Margaret could feel her face heat, and color flushed her cheeks. It was almost as if Andy could read her mind. The only thing on her mind at that moment was to get out of there as fast as possible. Avoiding Andy's eyes by fumbling for her keys, she edged her way toward the door. Composing herself, Margaret left with, "Call if you need anything."

Andrew went into the kitchen to find something to eat. He looked at the white cupboards, white countertops, and white appliances. It looked clean, but Andrew couldn't help thinking about the contrast between this kitchen and Nan's kitchen. The farm cupboards were oak, darkened by years of use. The floor was also wood but polished to a high gloss. He shook his head and thought, *Your kitchen was so warm and inviting, Nan.* Andrew opened two cans of chicken noodle soup and put them on the stove to simmer. He sat down at the table and noticed tears in Andy's eyes as he sat in front of a plate that was empty except for a trace of dried syrup. "Oh, Papa, it was supposed to be such a wonderful day. Dad said it was the day I would start thinking about life differently, more grown-up, you know?"

"That has certainly come true today, son. One day you will look back on today and realize it was a day of both great sorrow and wonder. Your heavenly Father has given me your guardianship, but he has made it very clear that today he will be in charge of your training and lead you where he wants you to go."

"How do you know that? Dad always said I needed to ask what God has to say about something before I can be sure it's true."

"Your dad was right. Let's find out what God has to say about this." Andrew went into the living room and picked up the well-read family Bible resting on the table beside his son's favorite chair. Fighting back tears that reflected his own breaking heart, he whispered, "Lord, I feel like you are trying to get some real important instructions to me and Andy, so if it's okay with you, can I ask you to put grieving on hold for a bit?" Eating was forgotten for the moment, so Andrew turned the burner off and sat down in the chair next to Andy.

Andrew bowed his head and said, "Father, you told me that all I needed to know had already been given. Lead me now to the words we need to hear; allow your Holy Spirit to feed our souls with the food you spoke of when you said that man did not live by bread alone."

Andrew was very still and quiet for what seemed a very long time to Andy. Andy cocked his head to one side and opened one eye to little more than a squint to see what his grandfather was doing. Andrew did not move but waited on the Lord with eyes closed and head bowed. Andy followed his grandfather's lead, bowed his head, and closed his eyes.

"We will start in John, Andy." Andrew's statement was so sudden that Andy opened his eyes with a start.

"What did you say?"

"We will start in John, the fourteenth chapter, seventeenth verse." Andrew opened his son's Bible and read, "And I will ask the Father, and he will give you another Counselor to be with you forever."

"What do you think that means to me, Papa?"

"Exactly what it says. Your counsel will come from your heavenly Father."

"But God talks and leads everyone who asks him, reads the Bible, and does what they know is pleasing to him, right?"

"That's right, but there is more. The Word tells us that 'many are called but few are chosen.' We don't know what this means in every circumstance. But right here, at this moment, I have a pretty good idea that Matthew 22:14 is real personal."

"Wait a minute. My Bible says 'many are *invited* but few are chosen.' Is there any difference?"

"There may be some words that do make a difference, but in this case, the word that was translated was *kletos,* meaning 'to call or invite, or appoint.'"

"Does that mean I'm special to God?"

"Of course you're special. But so is the worst sinner. God is not a respecter of persons, and he patiently waits for all men to come to repentance. He doesn't want anyone to perish… (2 Peter 3:9).

"You see, God calls everyone. Those that choose salvation choose God. Then God uses some who have a heart for Christ to carry out specific plans, reach specific people, or go to specific places. I believe we are being told that you are one of these people. But for now, let's see what else God has for us."

Andrew again bowed his head and began to wait on the Lord's instruction. Andy cleared his throat in a manner that he knew would get his grandfather's attention. Andrew looked at Andy, expecting the question. Andy asked, "What are you doing when you're quiet? Are you praying?"

"No. I am obeying God's Word. It says in Exodus that 'The Lord will fight for you; you need only to be still.' It is so important for you to know God's Word so that God's Spirit will bring the wisdom you need when you need it. But your part is to know how to ask."

"I was doing okay up to now, but you just lost me."

"There are so many choices a person has in most circumstances. How do you know which one God wants you to take? If someone does something mean, do you do something mean back or get revenge in some way or maybe take them to court? I will admit that there may be a time for legal action, but first you need to be still before the Lord and wait patiently for him; do not fret when men succeed in their ways, when they carry out their wicked schemes (Psalm 37:7).

"How do you feel about being called for something special, Andy?"

Andy didn't answer. He felt a wave of deep sorrow, buried his face in the crook of his arm on the table, and began to cry. Andrew stayed quiet and put a reassuring hand on Andy's shoulder. He silently asked the Lord to give Andy the strength he needed to get through this.

When the pain was bearable, Andy looked up at Andrew and said, "I'm not sure I want to do special things for God. Why would he leave me alone at this time of my life?"

"I don't have an answer for you right now, but when the time is right, you'll know. I do know that our ways are not God's ways, and all we can do is trust that He knows what He's doing and we need to trust Him."

"That's not good enough, Papa. Why would I want to trust a God that would let a kid's parents get killed on his birthday?"

"Let's get through the next few days, and when you're ready we'll talk."

"There is one thing, Papa; I am going to make the arrangements for Mom and Dad. Their funeral will be at the church, not a funeral parlor."

Andrew nodded his head and answered, "Good for you."

· ·

The next two days were busy and hard for Andy and Andrew. Their evening talks had helped Andy soften his attitude toward God, and periods of grief were less frequent. Matt and Margaret came by to see if there was something they needed but never stayed long. Margaret was glad that she wasn't making the funeral arrangements for Harold and Sarah. Andy and Andrew enjoyed talking about the past and present, but Andy was reluctant to talk about the future.

Saturday night arrived. Andy and Andrew finished dinner and sat at the kitchen table. "I'm glad Pastor Frank agreed to a Sunday afternoon funeral, Papa. It really seems right that Mom and Dad will be in the church on Sunday and that will be the place their friends and family say their last good-byes. I'm really dreading tomorrow, though. My heart hurts," Andy said.

"I know, Andy. Mine hurts too."

"You don't seem to hurt as much as I do. Is that true?"

"In a way, I guess that is true, son. I know how happy your folks are, and that makes it easier for me to accept their death. You see, the hurt is all ours, not theirs."

Andy couldn't respond to these words. All he knew was how much he missed his parents. "I think I'll turn in early. I just wish there was something that could help the hurt."

"There is. This is where knowing the Word comes in. You have all of God's weapons, but a good soldier knows when to depend on the sword, when the breastplate is the best defense, or maybe just when moving away is the best tactic, because we are also told to have our feet fit with the readiness that comes from the gospel of peace. For right now, think about the breastplate. It's there to protect the heart. We will study and learn together, son, just like you and your dad."

With this, the Lord allowed his two children to begin healing again by bringing to mind the events that brought grandson and grandfather together. They stood to walk into the living room but fell into each other's arms, and rocking back and forth, they cried with loud sobs, knowing that their Lord was weeping and rocking with them.

Chapter Six

Warmed by the sun coming through his bedroom window, Andy realized he was awake but was reluctant to open his eyes. This was not a day he wanted to begin, and he heard himself whisper, "Can't we just wait a little longer, Lord? I'm not really ready to bury Mom and Dad yet." He knew that all the arrangements had been made and today would be the last day he could look into the double casket he had ordered and see his parents sleeping. He had instructed the mortician to have Harold's arm under and around Sarah and Sarah's head resting on his dad's shoulder. This was the way he almost always found them on Saturday and Sunday mornings when he was up first and woke them up to start the day.

Andy decided to stay where he was and let his mind talk to God. *I'm going to talk to my heavenly Father like Papa does. What was it Papa called him? Abba? He said Abba was like when we said "daddy," but I don't think I'm ready for that yet.* Andy started with *Father, so much has happened these past few days. I can't even remember some of it. Today is going to be so hard, but I wanted to thank you for having Grandpa Andrew here.* Andy continued in little more than a whisper, "Could you talk to me like you talk to Papa, Lord? If I'm real quiet and still, will you let me know that you really are here and can make everything okay? I don't think I can get through today if I'm not sure you are with me." Andy lay very still and tried to focus his mind on nothing but the name of Jesus.

Don't be afraid, little one; I'm here. "No one will be able to stand up against you all the days of your life. As I was with Moses, so I will be with you; I will never leave you nor forsake you" (Joshua 1:5). Then Andy's soul heard, "So do not fear, for I am with you; do not be dismayed, for I am your God. I will strengthen you and help you; I will uphold you with my righteous right hand" (Isaiah 41:10).

Andy sat up, and for a second thought he had heard Andrew. "Papa, did you say something?" He waited a minute to hear Andrew's response. When none came, he shouted, "Papa, are you there?" When Andy still didn't hear his Grandpa Andrew's voice, he looked around the room and whispered, "Was that you, Lord?"

Yes, Andy.

Andy thought for a minute and realized that he had heard the Lord sure enough to answer but hadn't really heard a sound, so he asked, "How come I can hear you but you're not making any sound?"

Because you hear me with your spiritual ears, Andy. My Word says that the time will and has come when true worshipers will worship me in spirit and truth. I remind you in that scripture that I am spirit, so you must worship me in spirit.

"How come I never heard you before this?" Andy whispered.

Because you didn't know how to listen. People get so busy doing *things for me,* learning *about me, and* petitioning *me to meet their needs that they are too noisy or busy to hear me answer. To the world, my voice is still, so the world can't hear me, and many of my children won't hear me. But if you meet me in the spirit, I can sound like a thousand clashes of thunder and still be understood.*

Andy thought he heard laughter in the Lord's voice and decided to ask him as a test to see if he was still asleep. He felt a little sheepish but figured he didn't have anything to lose, so he said aloud, "Were you being funny, Lord?"

There was humor in what I said. When the time comes, ask Moses or Job or Isaiah about thunder. I used it several times to get the attention I needed to get my point across. The Lord responded again with the ring of humor in his voice.

Andy sat very still so he wouldn't miss one word. The conversation stopped, and Andy realized that he felt very comfortable in the silence. It wasn't long before he felt tears running down his face as he remembered what he had to do today. "How will I get through this, Father? How can I watch them lower Mom and Dad into the ground?" Andy whispered between sobs.

I will give you the strength you need to get through today, Andy. But remember that you only bury the likeness of your parents. They are here with me. They have new bodies, new names, and a new purpose—a joy beyond your understanding. You will also know these things when you finish your journey and come home.

Andy was filled with awe and smiled as he looked up toward heaven with a heart so full he didn't know whether to laugh or cry. He shouted, "Oh, thank you! Thank you, Abba! You have given me a strength I've never felt before. I have been filled with a need to worship and yet find no words worthy of what needs to be said. Even in this bitter time, I can bow to your wisdom and accept the plate you have prepared for me."

Andy showered and dressed in record time and ran downstairs to share everything the Lord had said with Papa. Andrew was sitting in the kitchen with God's Word open, and he grinned from ear to ear when Andy bounced into the kitchen shouting, "Just wait till I tell you what happened to me this morning, Papa! It was great!"

Andrew threw his head back and laughed from the bottom of his soul. "I know it was, Andy. I can see it in your face. Now sit down and tell me what happened while I fix you some breakfast."

Andy told his papa everything and finished at the same time he took his last bite of cornflakes. Once again, grandfather and grandson bowed in adoration and love for the giver of all great and wonderful gifts. Andrew, remembering God's Word, told Andy that the Lord had given him a great gift and "A gift opens the way for the giver and ushers him into the presence of the great" (Proverbs 18:16).

"You have given the Father a gift he patiently waits for all his children to give, Andy. The gift of your awareness will indeed usher you into the presence of the great."

"Hold it, Papa. You just lost me again. What's the gift of awareness, and how can I give anything to God?"

"Just be aware of him in everything you do. It is one of the things God will not do for you. The Lord is delighted when his children use their will to remember his word and expects his children to remind him of what he promised. You know how to love with your heart. The past few days have taught you that. Remember how your heart hurts when you think about not seeing your mom and dad here on earth anymore?"

"Yes. It hurts so bad sometimes I don't think it will ever stop."

"But it does for a while and comes back again when you have gained a little of your strength and you think about it again. Let me ask you something. Explain the breath you just took."

"That's not hard. I took air in then blew it out."

"That's right. You take each breath automatically, without thinking about it. You just do it, right?"

"Right again."

"But what if you had lung cancer or emphysema? Each breath of air would be so important that it would demand your full attention. Your awareness would have changed, and so would your priority and purpose."

"So what you are saying is that when we give God our full attention, we are giving him our awareness?"

"That is basically right. There is much more to it than that, but you have the basics. Are you going to Sunday service this morning?"

"I thought about it but think I'll just go to the church around two when they bring Mom and Dad from the funeral home. Do you mind?"

"Not at all. Do you want me to go down with you this afternoon or wait until three?"

"Actually, Papa, I'd like some alone time with Mom and Dad."

Andrew understood, as he had spent alone time with his son and daughter-in-law at the funeral home.

⦁ ⦁

Knowing that they would soon be in the presence of the Master, the Lord's warriors Nahal, Darak, and Lachotaam had spent the night in worship as Andy slept. They had put an angelic hedge around Andy so no evil influence could disturb his rest. Nahal stationed himself close to Andy's head, whispering praises and scriptures to the sleeping child.

Haphak had seen all this before and knew what was coming. The distress he felt was almost beyond endurance because he knew Satan also knew what was happening. He had watched as Nahal prepared Andy to receive the direction and manifestation of the Holy Spirit, and every effort he made to interfere was to no avail. He had been summoned by his master and was desperate for one small victory before the meeting. Haphak knew those ungrateful little demons he had brought with him on this important mission had wasted no time in letting Satan know about the failure. *What can I do to turn this around?* Haphak thought. *If this power takes possession and the boy learns that he can use and trust it, we may have lost the war for Andy.*

"Why are you still here, Haphak? I know you heard the master call." The words dripped from the mouth of Liar. Criticism, standing behind him, added, "You were bound to fail. You really aren't as good as you think you are."

Haphak's mind raced with thoughts of escape when it finally hit him. "Margaret! Why have I been standing around here all night? She's the answer. If anyone can get to Andy, she can." Haphak spun around, and with the authority he knew he still had, he commanded Liar and Criticism to go to Satan and tell him he was in the middle of a plan. Haphak was instantly standing in the Selby kitchen directly behind Margaret.

Chapter Seven

"It's only eight thirty! Two more hours before we can get this show started and over." Margaret spoke so suddenly it startled Matt.

"How can you be so cold, Margaret? He was your brother."

Margaret thought about how bad she must have sounded and tried to explain. "I'm sure when I have time to think about it my loss will hit home. Right now I'm overwhelmed with the accident, the legal papers, and routing all my other work to paralegals and other lawyers. The most difficult has been having to deal with Dad and Andy. That alone is almost more than I can handle."

"Did you give a copy of your instructions for the funeral to your dad?"

"Yes, but the frown on his face when he read them told me there would be changes."

"Like what?"

"Apparently, Andy went to the funeral home and left his own instructions. He is going to have Sarah and Harold moved to the church for the service. He wants an open casket, and the three o'clock service will be announced during the worship service this morning. I don't understand why they couldn't have had the service at the mortuary."

"You're being unreasonable. The church was a big part of your brother, Sarah, and Andy's lives."

Margaret didn't answer but thought to herself, *Yes, but I can't control the service. If there was any way I could get out of going and save face in this town, I would. But Matt's right; he was my brother, and for some reason, it seems like everyone knew him.* It was so strange at times like this when Margaret seemed to listen to her thoughts rather than think them. Instead of worrying about it, she leaned back with her coffee and indulged in how hard it had been on her to juggle her time between Matt, work, Andy, and her dad. *What do I get for all my effort? I get to go to church. This thing will be like a Sunday sermon, except Harold will be lying in a coffin instead of sitting in a pew.* Margaret smirked as she thought about Harold saying that he would get her to go to church someday. *Well, you were right, little brother; I just didn't think you would go this far to get the job done.*

Margaret thought about the last funeral she had attended and asked, "Matt, do they always do this thing where anyone who wants to talk about the deceased can just stand up and start talking?"

"I don't think they do that at every funeral, but you might want to call your dad and ask if they plan to do that at the church."

As she headed toward the phone, she said, "I'll do that. Just can't imagine how I will endure a sermon from Pastor Frank. And then if Dad stands up, he will feel the need to quote half the Bible." Margaret stopped and put her hand up to her mouth. "You don't think Dad will allow Andy to stand up and make a fool of himself at the funeral, do you?"

Matt just looked at Margaret with two raised eyebrows and shrugged.

Margaret dialed her brother's now-familiar phone number. After Harold died, she had to look up the number and write it down. Since her dad had arrived, it seemed like she had dialed the number several times a day and now knew it by heart.

"Staple residence." It was Andy's voice, but it sounded like he was laughing.

"Is that you, Andy?"

"Oh, hi, Aunt Margaret. Yes, it's me. What's up?"

Margaret decided she must be mistaken about Andy's tone and asked if her father could come to the phone for a minute. Margaret heard, "Sure, hold on." Then she heard a very loud, "Papa! It's Aunt Margaret, and she wants to talk to you."

"Good morning, Maggie. Didn't the Lord give us a beautiful day?"

"Er…uh…yes. I guess so, Dad. Does the Baptist church let anyone stand up and talk about the deceased at a funeral?"

"They do if that is the wish of the family. Why?"

"Oh, I was just wondering if you had said anything to the pastor about the type of service you wanted and if that was included."

"As a matter of fact, Andy talked to the pastor and asked him to set aside some time for people to publicly say their good-byes to Sarah and Harold if they wanted to. Is that a problem?"

Margaret swore under her breath but managed a bright, "Oh, no. I was just wondering about the timing. With the service at the church, then the graveside service, and everyone going to Harold's house afterwards for potluck, the whole day is pretty well shot."

"You're right. Today has been set aside for the families to remember, reflect, and say good-bye to Sarah and Harold."

Margaret felt her cheeks burn and was thankful that she was talking to her father on the phone so he couldn't see her embarrassment. She knew she had sounded petty and had been reprimanded for it.

Margaret was determined to save face and lied, "Of course today is set aside, but a client wanted to know if I would be free for a meeting later on this evening, so I thought I'd check before giving her an answer. It looks like I need to set the appointment up for next week."

⸱ ⸱ ⸱ ⸱ ⸱ ⸱ ⸱ ⸱ ⸱ ⸱ ⸱ ⸱ ⸱ ⸱ ⸱ ⸱ ⸱

The Baptist church was one of the larger churches in the area. One of the church's deacons watched for the family so he could direct them to a special side room viewing area prepared for family who preferred privacy. Matt and Margaret arrived and were ushered to the side room. Sarah's mother and sister were sitting in the first row of chairs. Margaret was a bit irritated that the front row had not been reserved for Harold's family, even though there were more than enough chairs to accommodate both families in the first row of seats.

Sarah's sister stood up and, extending her hand, said, "You're Margaret, Harold's sister, aren't you?"

"Yes, I am. And this is my husband, Matt Selby."

"You probably don't remember us; we've only met a couple of times over the years. I'm Patricia Lowe, Sarah's sister, and this is our mother, Nancy."

Margaret reached over and shook Nancy's hand before sitting down in a chair that left two empty seats between her and Patricia.

There was a very good view of the church and the open casket sitting in the front and to one side of the center aisle. Nancy began sobbing quietly, and Patricia put her arm around her mother's shoulder. Patricia turned toward Matt and Margaret and asked, "Was it your idea to have a double casket built for Sarah and Harold?"

"No. That was Andy's idea," Margaret offered.

Nancy wiped her eyes. "What a comfort for Andy to remember his mother and father together like that."

Andrew walked into the room and smiled at Margaret as he walked toward Nancy. He took a chair from the back row and moved it beside Nancy and sat down next to her.

"Is there anything I can do, Nancy?" Andrew said as he took her hands in his and held them very firmly.

Nancy looked up at him with tear-reddened eyes. "No, Andrew. Jesus, our Lord, has taken the sting out of the death of Sarah and

Harold. I weep out of self-pity because I will no longer be allowed to hug Sarah until I join her in heaven."

Andrew smiled and, giving Nancy's hand a squeeze, said, "It is truly a glorious day for our children, Nancy."

Margaret sat with her mouth open in amazement at what she was hearing. Matt was a bit taken aback too but just gave Margaret a quick jab with his elbow when he saw the look on her face. Margaret knew the jab meant, *Just shut your mouth, grit your teeth, and keep quiet.*

"Where is Andy, Dad?" Margaret finally managed when she calmed down.

"He's sitting in the front row of the church. He said he wanted to be closer to his mom and dad, and he also wanted to be available if someone wanted to talk to him."

"I can understand him wanting to be close to Harold and Sarah, but why on earth would he want to let people talk to him at a time like this?"

Andrew gave Nancy a quick glance, and she returned a look that let Andrew know she understood.

Andrew met Margaret's glare and said, "It is very sad that you do not understand that those people out there are Andy's church family, Margaret. They give him the strength he needs to get through this."

Margaret knew that she had again been reprimanded and had had enough. A bit louder than she intended, she said, "And what are we? Some kind of strangers that don't deserve to be included in his inner circle? After all, Dad, we are his *real* family."

Andrew knew Margaret was being defensive, and as gently as possible, he said, "Yes, we are, and that is very important to Andy. However, before the end of this service, I think you will understand why we couldn't give Andy what he needs today."

"What do you mean, 'by end of this service'? Surely Andy isn't going to say anything out there."

"On the contrary. Andy is going to conduct the whole service."

The organ began playing very softly. Margaret was more than a little impressed when she saw that not only were all the pews filled but the glass doors leading to the vestibule had been opened for additional rows of chairs. When these were filled, people began standing in the aisles, and the overflow extended outside the double doors that had been propped open. Margaret started to say something to Matt when she heard Andy's voice loud and clear from the loudspeaker directly behind them.

"Do you remember how it felt when you were told that someone you loved was going to come see you and when you asked when, the answer was 'soon'? I'm not sure anyone really knows exactly when 'soon' is, but when you're very young, it means 'right now.'" Andy smiled when he heard a few knowing chuckles. "Each passing day brings the same question about the arrival time, and each day the answer is the same. One day you're told that the loved one has some things to do to get ready and as soon as they finish those things, they will get to come see you."

Andy paused and then continued, "I believe that is the way the Lord feels the minute one of his loved ones is born. He is so anxious for that soul to come to him that he counts the years, days, minutes, and seconds, which he has predestined, until he can pull the loved one to himself. He waits because we each have things to accomplish before we can leave. Sometimes the difficulty is finding out what those things are. Sadly, sometimes we know what those things are and just don't want to do them, or we put it off for a very long time." Again, Andy paused for a second and silently prayed, *Help me, Father.*

"Mom and Dad knew what they were supposed to do and worked very hard every day to complete their job. The reason they were put here is no secret to anyone who knew them because they shared their purpose with anyone who would listen. They were looked up to and respected in the church, neighborhood, and business communities."

Andy was pleased when he heard several people comment, "That's right," and saw many heads nod in agreement to his statement. He continued, "Oh, I know Mom and Dad were killed in an accident, but I also know that if God had not set that day and hour as their time to go home, we would not be here today. The point is, they shared Jesus with everyone God had lined up for them and even went after a few strays." Andy couldn't help giving his aunt Margaret the slightest smile when he added that.

"The Word tells us in Ecclesiastes 7:1 that 'a good name is better than fine perfume, and the day of death better than the day of birth.'" Andy pointed at his parents and added, "They knew this and got their reputations through knowledge of God's Word. They believed Psalm 73:24, where it says, 'you guide me with your counsel, and afterward you will take me to glory.' They also knew that Psalm 116:15 was true that, 'precious in the sight of the LORD is the death of his saints.' Some of you have said to me today that Mom and Dad loved life, and that's very true, but Mom and Dad were *in love* with life everlasting.

"There is one physical death but two ways to look at it. We can choose death without sting in victory, or we can choose the dread that comes when man realizes he waited too long and all is lost. The man and woman God gave me as parents were true and much-loved children of our heavenly Father, and he said, 'Harold and Sarah, your time of interaction, play, and work is over. It's time to come home to supper,' and he called them home. I'm also sure that he comforted them by reminding them that he was the first fruit, that he had gone before them into this experience we call death, and there was nothing to fear as they stepped from temporary life into everlasting life."

Andy was finished and returned to his front-row seat shrouded in a silence that he didn't understand. There had to be well over a thousand people inside the church, not counting the ones in the vestibule, but it was as quiet as if the church was completely empty. Even Pastor Frank didn't move to the podium but sat with his head bowed and eyes closed. Andy just sat there and resisted the urge to look around to see if he could see the reason why everyone was so quiet.

After a few more minutes that seemed like an hour, Pastor Frank walked to the podium and said, "Let's pray." Pastor Frank was silent again, and Andy wondered if he was trying to think of something to say. Finally Pastor Frank began, "Heavenly Father, your Word has again touched our hearts and minds to understand life—life here in flesh and life everlasting with you. We remember that our Savior, Jesus Christ, took the sting and victory from death, and death became the doorway from one life to the next. We hold to your truth in Romans 14:7–8, where we are told, 'For none of us lives to himself alone and none of us dies to himself alone. If we live, we live to the Lord; and if we die, we die to the Lord. So, whether we live or die, we belong to the Lord.' As we bid farewell to the earthly presence of our brother Harold and sister Sarah, we gladly give that presence up to you. We give thanks that these precious souls have completed their journey through the desert, came to the Jordan, and entered the promised land. If there are any that have come today to honor the life that Harold and Sarah lived and do not know that they will someday see them again, we ask your Spirit to speak to their hearts and prepare them to accept the everlasting life you offer those that come to you. We pray by and with the authority of the name above all names, Jesus Christ. Amen. If there is anyone who would like to say something about Harold and Sarah, please come to the front."

People started lining up to give their public good-byes to Sarah and Harold. Margaret was amazed at how many people said how much they had helped them get through rough financial and emotional times. It sounded like whenever there was someone who needed help, Sarah and Harold were there.

When the last person spoke, people started walking by the casket and going outside to allow those who were not in the church room to come in. Margaret followed the first group outside.

Margaret was irritated that she could not control the tears that rolled down her cheeks. She didn't want to appear weak or vulnerable, and she sure didn't want to give her father a reason to say anything religious. She felt her father's soft, firm hand on her shoulder but resisted the impulse to shrug it off or look at him. This thought broke the spell, and Margaret realized she was again in control. As discreetly as possible, Margaret grabbed a tissue from her purse and wiped her eyes. She looked squarely into Andrew's eyes and said, "Allowing Andy to give the eulogy will probably be something that plagues him for the rest of his life. There is no telling what it will do to him. I hope you exercise better judgment in counseling Andy in the future."

Andrew gave a little chuckle as he answered, "You're right. This will no doubt stay with and influence Andy for the rest of his life. At least I certainly hope so. Margaret, didn't you understand anything Andy said?"

"I understood everything perfectly." Margaret was going to stop with that but decided to let her father know exactly where she stood. "I understand that this is the way some people deal with loss. They just can't grasp the fact that when you die you simply cease to exist. The thing that most of these people have to hold on to is that they live their lives as do-gooders and lay down so the world can walk on them without complaining about it, so there has to be some sort of reward after they die. Honestly, Dad, I can't understand how you can really buy all this."

Margaret felt her cheeks grow hot with embarrassment when she looked around and realized that Sarah's mother and sister and Andy had heard every word she said. Sarah's mother and sister looked stunned, but even though he had tears brimming his eyes, Andy was smiling at his aunt. He walked over and took Margaret's hand. "Come on, Aunt Margaret. Let's go put Mom's and Dad's bodies to rest." He led the way to a waiting car.

Andy's mind went to a house of memory. He vaguely remembered the ride to the cemetery, the closed casket, and praying, and then he realized he and his grandfather were the only ones sitting under a big, blue canopy the funeral home had put up over the gravesite. He looked at his papa and whispered, "I wish I could have been there to see the look on Dad's face when he saw Jesus. Knowing Mom, she probably just fell down and worshipped him. But Dad...I bet he had a thousand questions he was dying to ask." Andy chuckled and added, "No pun intended."

Andrew threw his arms around his grandson. They sat there for awhile neither saying anything. Andrew broke the silence with, "We'd better get to the house, Margaret won't know what to do with all those people."

"You're right papa, it just seems like this part of the whole thing is so final and I hate for it to end."

"I know but now we concentrate on the future and the living son, God has taken care of your folks."

* * * * * * * * * * * * * * * * * *

Pastor Frank was saying grace over tables of food that made Thanksgiving dinner look like a snack. Margaret looked up when she heard the front door open and close. Her look told them what they both knew would happen; Margaret was furious.

When the prayer ended, Frank asked Andrew if there was anything he would like to say. Andrew walked toward one table. "Thank all of you for being here. Let's eat."

A few guests came up to shake Andrew's hand and hug Andy. Andy was trying to be brave, but after several hugs, he thought a plate full of food might save him additional embraces. Andy thought, *I wish some of them would just shake my hand like they do Papa.* As soon as Mrs.

Ariel's hug ended, he ran to the table to grab a plate. To his delight, it seemed to be working.

Half of those present had filled plates, and at least a half a dozen women from the church were bustling back and forth from the kitchen to the dining room. Margaret knew this was her best chance to escape. She didn't want her departure to look cruel, but she was afraid her anger would cause her to do something worse. She waited for the opportunity and motioned to her father to follow her into Harold's small office. Andrew excused himself and closed the door after he stepped into the office.

Before Margaret could say anything, Andrew began, "This should be a day of sorrow for you, not anger. You have been angry since our telephone conversation this morning. Would you like to talk about what is bothering you or drop it and let me guess?"

Margaret stood with her face contorted with anger, arms folded in front of her, and her feet in a boxer's stance. The dam in Margaret's mind broke, and she began by swearing at her father. Then she continued, "I cannot believe today. First you allow a seventeen-year-old boy to deliver his parents' eulogy to a crowd of well over a thousand people. He stood up there and delivered a message that sounded like he was almost glad Sarah and Harold died. Then you make me come back here to be the hostess to…how many…one hundred, two hundred people that I don't even know. If I weren't so involved in my law firm, I would seriously consider finding an alternative to allowing Andy to remain under your custody."

Up to the last statement, Andrew was willing to let Margaret blow off steam, but he shot back before she could catch her breath. "Now you wait just one minute, little missy. I've tried to respect your belief, or lack of it, but you are on the verge of finding out that there are some situations when a Christian does not turn the other cheek." He stopped to let what he had said sink in then added, "You sure you're ready to take me on, Maggie?"

Margaret's mind began swirling with disconnected thoughts. Margaret had found out that Harold had left a substantial amount of money, and there was no indication that Andrew knew about it, but she wasn't sure. She was also truly concerned that her dad was too old to take on the responsibilities she knew would come. Margaret's comments were meant, in part, to see how her dad would react to the possibility of her and Matt taking Andy and to see if he would give any indication he knew about the money. Margaret opened her mouth, ready to challenge her father's authority once and for all, but no matter what she did, all she could do was stammer. She stopped trying to speak, and it was apparent by her expression that her anger had been replaced with frustration.

"Margaret, you have been under a lot of strain the past few days. I know how hard it can be to try to control situations that are completely out of our control. I did this with your mother for many years. She never condemned me but knew I felt condemned. She never got angry and fought with me, though she knew it would have been better for me if she had. She always let me know how much she loved me, knowing full well I didn't feel deserving. In short, her love, prayers, and smiles convicted me more than any courtroom trial." He started to put his arm around his little girl but decided against it. "That's where you are now. You have condemned yourself and can't find anyone to blame, and that's so frustrating that you want to lash out at anything or anyone."

Margaret's emotions were so worn that all she could do was sob. She thought, *You can't be serious. You know he thinks he broke through and touched a nerve that exposed your weaknesses. Straighten up, Margaret, and start acting like a lawyer instead of a three-year-old that's just been scolded.* "Let's not fight about this dad. We both want what's best for Andy. I just think he is under more strain than he realizes and may regret some of his decisions and words later. Frankly, I'm also a little concerned that you haven't seen this and exerted more authority over his actions. After all, he is only seventeen."

Andrew felt that he was being cautioned and needed to respond to Margaret very carefully. He took just a second to ask God for wisdom then said, "We both need time to think about this. Now is not the time. Can we discuss this tomorrow?"

Margaret knew Andrew was right but hated to concede. She felt as if she had the upper hand for the first time since her dad arrived and didn't want to lose the advantage she thought she had. She opened her mouth to tell him that this was a subject she didn't feel should be put off, but she said, "You're right, Dad. Now is not the time." She knew the look on her face was one of surprise. That was not at all what she had intended to say. She wondered what in the world was going on in her mind. Finally, while she collected her jacket and purse, she said, "I'll call you tomorrow and set up some time for us to meet."

All Andrew could do was whisper, "Thank you, Lord."

The last guest left around 8:30 p.m. It had been a long day. Andy and Andrew sat in a kitchen that had been cleaned and polished by the ladies from the church. The refrigerator was full of enough leftovers to last them a week, and the house suddenly became so quiet they could hear the clock in the living room. Andy broke the silence with, "Aunt Margaret was really mad, wasn't she?"

"You know, Andy, it's more than that. I sense that Maggie is in for more trouble than she ever dreamed possible. She is playing with an unquenchable fire. We need to pray for her. She is going to need some powerful protection, or she won't make it."

"What are you talking about?"

Andrew prayed for guidance about how or if he should tell Andy what he had seen in Margaret's eyes when she tried to get him to commit to something he knew would be a mistake. "Your Aunt Margaret is fighting a battle with herself. She knows that the Lord wants to take control of her life, but she thinks that if she lets that happen, she will lose."

"Lose what? What is more important than the Lord?"

"Maggie thinks she will lose the respect of the business world, which gives her a lot of clients, which means a lot of money for her and Matt. She thinks she has reached the position she has on her own, and nothing could be further from the truth. There are also battles going on in Margaret about her mother and the way she was raised that only she can work through."

"But she has worked hard to get where she's at, hasn't she?"

"That's right. But it's God who determines who is rich and who isn't. If it was God's will or way, he could take everything away in a quick second. What's worse for people who put their trust in fame and fortune is that they will lose it to someone or something else. King Solomon and Job were two of the richest men of their day, and Solomon said, 'God gives wisdom, knowledge, and joy to those who please him. But if a sinner becomes wealthy, God takes the wealth away and gives it to those who please him. Even this, however, is meaningless, like chasing the wind' (Ecclesiastes 2:26). Job said that you can collect silver like dust and piles of clothes only to lose it to the righteous. You can read what it says in Job 27:16–19."

Andrew went on to explain that some people think their wealth allows them to do whatever they please and no one would dare call their actions wrong. Turning to Hosea 12:8–9, Andrew showed Andy that it was what Ephraim thought. "Ephraim boasts, 'I am very rich; I have become wealthy. With all my wealth they will not find in me any iniquity or sin.' But listen to this: in verse nine, God says, 'I am the LORD your God, [who brought you] out of Egypt; I will make you live in tents again, as in the days of your appointed feasts.'"

"Would God really do that to Aunt Margaret and Uncle Matt?"

"The word isn't *would*. The word man must believe is *could*. People who depend on money and reputation don't get there by themselves.

In Psalm 73:3–12, we're told of a man who envied rich people because he saw the arrogance their prosperity afforded them. He says the rich never had to struggle and they were healthy and strong."

"But that's true, Papa. The rich do get all the breaks."

"That's right. Some do for a time, and unfortunately, others see that the wealthy are exempt from the troubles of life, so they try to attach themselves to rich or influential people instead of trusting in the Lord, thinking that their association with the rich will save them from trouble too." Andrew stopped and closed his eyes for a minute and thought about his precious Maggie. Andy hoped this lesson hadn't ended but had learned to be quiet and respectful when his grandfather was silent. Andrew looked at Andy and knew he was waiting for more information on this subject. He also saw something that pleased him deeply: a hunger for knowledge.

Andrew smiled and reached for Andy's young hands, holding them tightly as he continued. "The problem is that the day will come when the wealthy realize that their money can't save them from trouble."

Andy looked at his grandfather and said, "Why is Aunt Margaret in trouble? I know she knows about Jesus."

Andrew thought he had bypassed the real issue but realized that Andy needed an answer to his question. He took a deep breath, asked for wisdom, and as softly and unassuming as possible said, "Because she is allowing herself to be influenced by Satan."

Andy sat very still and quiet. He thought about what his grandfather had just said and wondered how he could respond or if he should. Andy looked into his grandfather's eyes and saw deep sadness and a touch of fear. He knew the fear was not for himself but for his daughter. All he could say was, "Let's pray for Aunt Margaret, Papa. Okay?"

Andrew bowed his head and suddenly felt very tired. He rested his elbows on the table and cupped his forehead with both hands. His tears were so abundant and came so fast that they splashed on the kitchen table. Andy scooted his chair over next to his papa's and put his arm around Andrew's shoulders. Not being sure what to do in a case like this, Andy prayed, "Help us help Aunt Margaret, God. Please help us."

Chapter Eight

The morning sun warmed the body and helped calm the spiritual turmoil Andrew had felt the night before. After spending time with God, he heard Andy bouncing down the stairs. He went straight for a bowl and a box of cornflakes.

"You sure that's all you want this morning, Andy?"

"Yeah. I'm not really that hungry. I ate enough food yesterday to last me awhile," Andy said with a grin.

"I'm going to visit an old friend of mine in town. Wanna go along?" Andrew asked.

"I would really like to just stay home today. The past few days haven't given me much time to think things out. Do you mind?"

"Not a bit. I won't be gone long." Andrew checked his pockets for the keys to his rental. "You know, I should turn the rental in. We can use Harold's car. Would that bother you?"

"No. It's kinda dumb to pay for a car when there are two cars sitting in the garage."

Andrew went to the phone and dialed Margaret's number. Matt answered on the second ring.

"Hello."

"Hello, Matt. You know, I didn't stop to think that this was a workday for you. How come you're home?"

"Oh, hi, Andrew." Matt chuckled a little and answered, "I think I spent too much time at the dessert table yesterday. Got just a bit of indigestion. What's up with you two?"

"We're both just fine. I was wondering if I could ask for a favor."

"Sure. What do you need?"

"Well, it occurred to me that with two cars sitting in the garage, it was a bit ridiculous for me to keep paying for a rental. I'm going into town and was wondering if Margaret would meet me at the airport and give me a lift back home at noon. I'd be willing to spring for lunch."

"Margaret's got a lunch meeting today, but I can pick you up. Under the circumstances, I'll pass on lunch."

"Are you sure? If you aren't feeling well, I can get a cab."

"I'm fine, Andrew. As a matter of fact, I'd enjoy visiting with you. We haven't really had a chance to talk."

"Okay, if you're sure it won't be too much. Let's see, it's nine thirty now. How about if I meet you there in an hour?"

"No problem. See you at ten thirty."

As Andrew walked toward the door, he asked Andy one more time, "You sure you don't want to go?"

"I'm sure, Papa. Have fun. I'll be fine."

It took Andrew about ten minutes to drive to the security bank. He hadn't called ahead but thought that if his high school friend was busy, he could just say hello and arrange to meet later.

Bob Clark was talking to one of the tellers when Andrew walked into the bank. He walked up behind Bob, waited until he finished his conversation, and announced, "Is it possible for me to have a few minutes of your time, sir?"

"Of course," Bob said without really looking at the man who asked the question. Bob looked up as he extended his hand toward Andrew.

He squinted his eyes as he tilted his head a little to the left. "Andrew Staple, you old dog! I was wondering when we would have a chance to talk." Bob's tone changed quickly as he added, "I'm so sorry about Harold and Sarah. I can't tell you how much they will be missed. They were good people."

Taking Bob's hand for a firm handshake meant to make up for many lost years, Andrew answered, "Thank you, Bob. It's so good to see you again. Except for the hair, you haven't changed a bit."

"Let's go to my office." As they passed a middle-aged woman sitting at a beautifully polished desk outside a large glassed-in office, Bob asked, "Could you get two old codgers a cup of coffee, Jan?"

Jan started to get up to get some coffee when she looked up and saw Andrew standing there with a grin on his face. "You bet! But it will cost Andrew a big hug."

Andrew threw his arms open, more than happy to pay the bill. Andrew heard the sorrow in Jan's voice as she told him how much she would miss Sarah, who had been a good friend and sister in Christ. Andrew gave her an extra-loving squeeze and said, "I know, Jan. But be happy for them in their new home."

The two men sat in comfortable plush leather chairs behind the glass barrier that separated the bank president from the rest of the banking staff. "My, oh my, Bob. This is quite impressive. When did all this happen?"

"Several years ago. It's too bad we lost touch for so long, but now maybe we can see more of each other since you're taking over as executor of Harold's estate."

Andrew was quiet for a few seconds, his face showing deep thought. "Not sure what you mean, Bob. Margaret will be handling the financial distributions and settlements of Harold's account. But I have custody of Andy."

Now it was Bob's turn to deeply consider Andrew's words. He frowned. "Are you sure that's wise?"

"Well, she is a lawyer, and since Harold and Sarah gave her their wills, I assumed that handling their estate was something she would know more about than I would. Why?"

Bob hesitated again. "You couldn't know this, but Margaret's personal and business account is here at First Security."

"No, but I'm glad they are because they are in good hands."

"I cannot ethically say anything more on the subject except to caution you to think this through before you leave Harold's holdings in Margaret's care."

Bob's remark disturbed Andrew, but he knew better than to ask Bob for more information about Margaret's accounts. Changing the subject, Andrew asked, "What kind of money are we talking about, Bob? Is there enough to see Andy through high school and college?"

Bob looked a bit confused and answered, "You really don't know how much Harold was worth?"

"No, never really thought it was any of my business. Why?"

"Since you have custody of Andy, I can share this with you. Just a minute, let me get you some information." Bob pushed the intercom button, and Andrew heard Jan answer, "Yes, Bob?"

"Jan, will you print out a report on the Harold Staple account?"

In less than two minutes, Jan walked in with several sheets of paper.

Jan left the room, closing the door behind her. Bob studied the papers for a minute then took a red pen from his desk and made a large circle around a bottom figure. He handed the paper to Andrew, who automatically scanned the paper for the red circle his friend had just made. Shock was the only way to describe the look on Andrew's face.

"I had no idea we were talking about so much. How did all this happen?"

"Harold was a good steward. His time was spent doing the things he enjoyed, not trying to get rich. Guess he left that up to God. His generosity to those who needed his help always bothered me, but for some reason, they always turned out better for him in the end. Plus, he was a good businessman and made some very wise investments, including this bank. Add the house, shop, and his business to that figure, and I'd say Andy will have no financial problems for his future for many, many years."

"You're right about that." After a brief hesitation, Andrew added, "I'm still wondering about your concern about Maggie handling Andy's affairs. For reasons that have little to do with this money, I don't want to change this arrangement. What are my options here?"

"Well, what I can do since you are Andy's guardian and this really is his money is make sure you have an accounting of all transactions on this account. There are some papers you need to fill out that will put you on the account too."

"What do you mean, 'too,' since Harold's and Sarah's names are no longer valid?"

Before he answered, he made a brief call over the closed inter-com to Jan. "Jan, I need you to get the packet of necessary papers for Andrew to be included on Harold's account."

While they waited, Andrew picked up the remaining papers containing Harold's account information. This time, he found the first page and looked at the names on the account. He read *Harold or Sarah Staple* with the word *deceased* following their names. Then he read *Margaret Selby*. Andrew asked, "When did this happen?"

"Actually, the day of the accident, Margaret came to my office with all the legal papers she needed to add her name to the account. It surprised me when she asked me more than once if I was sure the information on Harold's account was correct. I don't think she knew her brother was a millionaire."

Again Jan entered the room. This time Jan handed Bob a gold and blue folder containing several cards, a passbook, and checks. Bob handed the folder to Andrew, saying, "You need to fill these out as soon as possible."

Andrew took the offered folder. "Can I get these back to you later? I have to meet Matt at the airport in about five minutes."

Standing up and offering his old friend his hand, Bob answered, "Of course you can, but better sooner than later, and give them to me personally."

Andrew put the folder down so he could use both of his hands to grasp Bob's outstretched hand. "Seeing you again and knowing you are giving my grandson's interests your personal attention means a lot to me, Bob. Thank you."

"I agree with the first part. I wouldn't have the second part any other way."

● ● ● ● ● ● ● ● ● ● ● ● ● ● ● ● ●

Andrew saw Matt's BMW parked at the receiving curb at the airport, so he drove up beside him and hit the automatic window button. Matt looked up as Andrew yelled, "Give me just a couple of minutes to turn this in. Sorry I'm late."

"No problem. Take your time."

In a very short time, Matt and Andrew were leaving the airport. Andrew explained that he had stopped by the bank and, meeting an old friend, time got away from him. "I was there longer than I planned. Were you waiting long?"

"No, just got there." Matt grinned and added, "Besides, I decided to just play hooky for the rest of the day."

"Great. I wish Maggie could learn to take time off and relax a bit more. She seems so intense."

"I talk to her all the time about that. She is very dedicated to her practice and, as a result, is very good at it."

"How about a cup of coffee, Matt? You can skip the donut."

Matt chuckled. "I'd enjoy that, but do you need to get back to Andy?"

"No, Andy said he needed some time alone. Things have been pretty hectic for that little guy."

Matt parked in front of the Donut House. The two men got some coffee and sat at a table next to a window. Beginning a conversation was a bit difficult, so they began with the usual small talk. Then Andrew said, "Margaret was upset about me allowing Andy to officiate at the funeral. I would be interested in knowing how you felt about that."

Matt waited to answer Andrew's question then said, "I thought it was okay. It surprised me that someone so young and emotionally involved had what it takes to talk to a group that size. Standing up in front of a group of any size is something most people can't do."

"And what did you think about what he said?"

Matt was not as uncomfortable or hostile as Margaret when it came to talking about spiritual matters. "There was a lot of depth and insight about what he said, but to be honest, I didn't reflect on his speech too much. You know that religion is a subject that Margaret views with a lot of sarcasm, and the result is not pleasant for anyone who brings it up. I've found that the best thing to do to keep peace in the family is to keep my thoughts on that subject to myself."

"I'm sorry to hear that. Maggie had a God-fearing and loving mother who taught her about Jesus when she was little. I am partly to blame for Maggie's hostility and have had to live with that knowledge for a long time."

"I don't understand. You are more Christian than anyone I know."

Andrew chuckled at Matt's emphasis on the word *Christian* and again said, "I'm sorry to hear that too. Knowing and having Christian friends is very important. But to answer your question, I wasn't always concerned about living for Christ. There was a time when, like Maggie, and I guess you too, Christ was a small part of my life and held no place in my heart. For me, the death of my sweet Nan turned me around, but it had the opposite effect on Maggie." After reflecting on that time of his life, Andrew continued his explanation. "You see, Matt, I used the farm as an excuse to keep me from helping Nan build a home that had Christ as the foundation. In short, I had made the farm an idol. Before Nan died, I called out to God to spare Nan. He didn't. After she died, I needed a comfort the world could not give me, so I started reading the Word and looking for answers. It was very interesting how Scripture takes on personal meaning when you look for answers to specific questions."

"I can't say I understand that. What do you mean?"

"One scripture that I held on to was, 'The Lord will judge his people and have compassion on his servants when he sees their strength is gone and no one is left, slave or free. He will say: "Now where are their gods, the rock they took refuge in?"' (Deuteronomy 32:36). It was then that I realized I had taken refuge from Nan and religion in the farm. My strength was gone, and I felt I was dying. It was at that point that there was a decision I had to make: continue on the way I was going or return to the Lord. I continued to search Scripture for answers and found Proverbs 1:23–2:5. This scripture simply says that I might have been spared a lot of heartache if I had listened to God when he called me through Nan. If you get a chance, read those verses; you will be impressed with how they can jump out and have a lot of meaning for you just when you need them."

"So that's when it started. You know, Margaret has shared a little of her childhood with me, but I never knew what had turned her so bitter about God stuff."

Again, Matt's descriptive words amused Andrew, but there was also sadness in the realization of how empty their lives were. Andrew silently asked God for guidance before he continued. "What's your Christian background, Matt?"

"Guess it's about the same as Margaret's, except my dad and mom went to church every Sunday and took me and my brother when we were little. They thought religion was a personal thing, though, and when we turned nine or ten, they sort of left it up to us to decide if that's the way we wanted to go. My brother liked church, and he still goes all the time. He even has prayer meeting at his house. He invites us over all the time, and I guess you know that turned Margaret off, so we don't really see them much."

"How do you feel about that?"

"I've learned to live with." As soon as the words left his mouth, Matt regretted his answer.

Andrew could sense Matt's discomfort and wondered if he should press him to talk about it. He finally decided to leave it up to Matt. "Would you like to talk about it? If not, I'll change the subject, but it sounds like Margaret's position on religion bothers you."

Matt felt like the conversation was on the edge of betrayal, but he knew that Andrew was not one to condemn, so he decided to take the subject one step further. "It bothers me that we've disconnected ourselves from our families. You know how little we saw Harold, and my brother is the only family I have left. Our friends are friendly if it's expedient for them. Our social life consists of parties geared to see and be seen by the *right* people, if you know what I mean."

"I know what you mean and can certainly understand why not seeing your brother would bother you. I assume you've tried to talk to Margaret about this?"

"In the beginning, yes. But Margaret made it clear that if I chose to, as she put it, 'hang around with those people,' she would give me my freedom so I could spend as much time with them as I wanted."

"Ouch! That is stronger than I realized." Andrew silently prayed for Matt and his situation. Not sure if he should continue, he threw out an open-ended question. "If there's any way I can help, Matt…you know I love you and Maggie, and you are both heading for some real hurt."

Matt looked at Andrew as if he had just been given a warning. "What do you mean by that?"

"I can't give you any details until some things I think are in the works play out, but be very careful about what you support, and don't be afraid to pray. Prayer is something that's between you and God, and no one else even needs to know you've asked God for guidance."

"You have me worried now, Andrew. Are you sure you can't give me a hint about what you're thinking?"

"No. I need to do a lot more praying about how to handle all that's happening so I can hopefully prevent anyone from getting hurt."

The two men sat in silence. Andrew finally said, "I need to get back to Andy. There are some decisions he needs to make about his future."

"Like what?"

"Where he wants to live for the time being, for one. He has his school here with all his friends and a real support network in his church, and he feels comfort being in the home he shared with Sarah and Harold."

"I see what you mean. I just assumed that you and Andy would be going back to the farm. What will you do with the farm?"

Andrew stood up to leave as he answered, "There is a family that moved into the small house to help me take care of the place, so I don't need to worry about the farm."

The drive home was relatively quiet. When they pulled into the driveway, Andrew asked Matt if he wanted to come in for a while. When Matt declined, Andrew extended his hand toward Matt. When Matt took Andrew's hand, Andrew covered Matt's hand with his free hand as if to say, *You have my love and support.* "Thanks again for the pickup, Matt."

"Anytime, Andrew. You can depend on me."

Andy was in the office playing a game on the computer designed to help build typing skill by blasting letters of the alphabet as they fell from the top of the screen before they reached the bottom. He heard the front door open and close and yelled, "Is that you, Papa?"

"Yes, Andy. Sorry I was gone so long. Matt and I decided to go have coffee and catch up."

Andrew went into the living room and sat down in Harold's chair to think about what he had learned that morning. Andy tried to hit each letter of the alphabet and knew the *q* and *z* were coming up, and these were the two letters that always caused him trouble. When the little finger of his left hand again let him down, Andy made a face and ended the game. He walked into the living room, and one look at Andrew's face told him there was something wrong.

"What's up, Papa?" Andy said as he sat down on the couch across from Andrew.

Andrew wasn't quick to answer Andy's question. He wasn't sure how to, or if he should, give Andy all the details about his folks' finances. *After all*, Andrew thought, *this is just a seventeen-year-old boy.* Andrew decided to find out how much Andy already knew and answered Andy's question with another question.

"Did Harold ever talk to you about finances, Andy?"

"Sure, all the time. Dad said all our blessings came from God but that he expected us to take care of it like it was a gift or something." Andy wanted to impress his grandfather, so he continued with, "Dad started an account in my name at the bank and made sure I kept the account current on the computer. One of the things I had to do was add up the deposits plus the interest and figure out what my tithe should be."

Andrew smiled as memories of when Harold was Andy's age worked their way to the present. Harold and Andrew sat at the kitchen table every Friday afternoon to update and balance the farm books. Harold was very meticulous about adding any income and entering expenses in the multi-column book. Andrew kept a careful eye on every entry, and Harold soon learned that when his dad asked him to check his figures again, there had been a mistake. It had become a valuable learning game with Harold trying to see how long he could go without Andrew finding a mistake and Andrew trying to catch a slip-up in Harold's entries. Andrew commented in barely more than a whisper, "Like father, like son."

"What was that?"

Andy's question brought Andrew's awareness back to the problem at hand. He smiled at Andy and answered, "Nothing important, Andy. It's just that I did the same thing with your dad."

"Yeah! Dad said you told him how important it was to understand the responsibilities of handling money."

"Did your dad ever discuss *his* finances with you?"

"A little…" Andy answered slowly, trying to remember something his father had said. Finally Andy jumped up and yelled over his shoulder, "Hang on a minute. Dad said that if anything should happen to him I was to look for an envelope taped under the top drawer of his desk and follow his instructions." Andy had forgotten about the envelope. He rushed into the office and was excited as he thought about reading something his dad had written to him and the prospect of a treasure hunt. Andrew became excited too and followed Andy into the office.

Andy ran to the desk and opened the top drawer. Getting down on his knees, he looked at the bottom of the drawer and found an envelope taped toward the back. He tore the envelope free, and before he opened it, tears that seemed to come from nowhere rolled down Andy's face. As he sat on the floor, he remembered the day his dad told him about the envelope.

Andrew sat down behind the desk and patiently waited. "It was just two years ago," Andy said aloud, "about a week after my fifteenth birthday, when Dad asked me to come into this office and told me about the bank account he had opened for me. That's when he told me that I would have to give an accounting of how I spent my money and about the envelope. He told me not to get the envelope unless something happened to him. I remember that I felt real scared when he said that to me."

Andrew just nodded, not wanting to break into Andy's memory.

Andy took another quick look at the envelope and slowly opened it as if it were a gift of great value. He unfolded the enclosed papers and read aloud:

> *Dear Son,*
>
> *If you are reading this, I have gone to my new life with the Lord. I know this must be a very hard time for you, but I'm sure Papa Andrew is there with you now, praying for you as you read this letter.*
>
> *Hopefully you are old enough to understand all that I'm about to tell you, but if not, just ask my dad. He will answer any questions you have and help you understand what you need to do.*
>
> *Let me say right off, son, you are a very wealthy young man.*

Andy stopped when he read this and looked at Andrew, who again gave a little nod of confirmation. Andy continued reading.

> *Because of time, expenses, and interest, which I know you under-stand, I cannot tell you exactly how much is in the accounts. I'm certain that Andrew has checked with the bank and can give you a reasonable accounting. Attached to this letter is a copy of my last will and testament and a small envelope addressed to Andrew. Give these to Papa for safekeeping, Andy. These are very important documents, and Papa will know what to do. Your Aunt Margaret also has a copy in her office, but this one is the original, signed by my hand and notarized. You may not fully understand all the legal things in my will, but it says that my dad is your legal guardian, and unless he dies, that cannot be changed for any reason. It says*

that Andrew is in charge of your money and has the right to spend it any way necessary.

It is not possible for me to be sad in heaven, Andy, but you are the one and only thing I would miss. Seeing your smile, watching you grow to maturity both physically and in the Lord, our talks, hugs, and most of all, the warmth of the love I was able to give and receive. Grow strong in the Lord, Andy. His love will always protect and guide you through anything that comes your way, and someday we will be together again.

All my love,

Dad

Andy's sobs were so loud and labored that Andrew quickly dropped to the floor next to Andy, took the boy in his arms, and gently rocked him as he allowed the hurt of a broken heart continue to mend.

He took comfort in knowing that God was in charge. Andy had thrown his arms around Andrew and held him as tight as a drowning man would hold a life preserver. Slowly Andy's sobs slowed to short whimpers, and he looked up at his papa and said, "I'm so glad you're here with me. Promise me you won't leave me too."

Andrew knew what Andy needed. "I can promise you this, Andy. As long as the Lord knows you need me, I'll be here with you." After a short pause he continued, "When the day comes for me to leave, you will be able to handle it."

Andy stood up and helped his grandfather up. Andrew sat down in the chair behind the desk, and Andy went around to the chair on the opposite side of the desk. After they sat down, Andy remembered the rest of the papers and handed all the contents of the envelope to Andrew. Andrew took the papers and found the smaller envelope addressed to him. He read at the top in bold letters: *Use your best judgment about how much of this to share and when. Critical information follows.* Andrew quickly scanned the letter and saw two asterisks toward the bottom. He also saw Margaret's name mentioned in this section and understood his son's wisdom. Andrew knew Andy was waiting for him to read the note, and he decided to read as far as the asterisks for now.

Father,

I regret that these responsibilities have fallen on your shoulders. We don't understand God's reason for his plan but know there is a plan and it's perfect. As his Word says, "Though he brings grief, he will show compassion, so great is his unfailing love. For he does not willingly bring affliction or grief to the children of men."

It is hard for Andy to understand this now, but in time and with your help, someday he will.

Mr. Don Realson is a close friend and an attorney and also has a copy of my will. Please contact him and go over the provisions I've made for you and Andy. As you know, Margaret is the executor of my estate, and I did this with the hope that lessons might be learned that will have an eternal effect on her and Matt.

I don't need to tell you to take good care of Andy and how important it is to constantly direct his path toward God. You know this better than I do.

All my love,

Your son, Harold

Andrew stopped reading. He had come to the two asterisks and wanted to read the remainder of the letter before deciding whether to share the contents with Andy. He folded the paper and put it in his shirt pocket to finish at a later time. Andrew said, "Do you want to read your father's will?"

"No. Like he said, I probably wouldn't understand it anyway, but could I have my letter from Dad? I'd like to keep it with me for a while."

Andrew stood up and walked around the desk. He handed Andy the letter addressed to him and gave Andy another hug, saying,

"Everything's going to be all right. Just trust God. Let's go into the living room, son. There are some things we need to talk about."

Andrew and Andy stopped by the kitchen, made two bologna sandwiches, opened a soda, and went back into the living room.

After a few bites, Andrew opened the conversation with, "How would you feel about staying here instead of moving to Portland, at least for the time being?"

Andy looked up from his sandwich, and a big grin spread across his face. "Oh, Papa, I was wondering how I would ask you if we could stay here. I was afraid it would hurt your feelings if you thought I didn't want to move to your house. I really don't want to leave here. Are you sure it's okay with you?"

"It makes sense to stay here. It will take awhile to settle your folks' estate. Your school and friends are here, and I like the church you go to. Besides, I'd like to spend more time with Matt and Maggie."

Andy doubled up his fist, thrust it in the air, and quickly bringing it down exclaimed, "Yes!" All Andrew could do was chuckle.

After a short period of silence, Andy asked, "How much money was Dad talking about, Papa? It sounds like there is quite a bit."

"Let me put it this way—I haven't got the exact figures because your dad had several investments and I don't know what they are, but the bottom line is you are a millionaire."

Andy had just taken a drink of his pop, and the news his grandfather just gave him resulted in his lap being sprayed with a fine mist of orange soda. "You have got to be kidding."

"No. I'm not kidding. God was very generous, and your dad invested very wisely."

As hard as he tried, Andy could not think of another thing to say. He just sat there and stared at Andrew.

Andrew finally smiled and added, "You better close your mouth; you'll catch flies." They both laughed at this and finished their lunch.

After they finished eating and took their dishes back to the kitchen, Andy said he was going to his room to listen to some music. Before he left the room, he asked, "Do you mind if I go to school tomorrow? I'd like to see what I've missed, see some of my friends, and let the school know I'm not going to be leaving for a while."

Knowing that he would have a lot of running around to do, Andrew answered, "I think that is a great idea, Andy."

Andy ran up the stairs to his room.

Andrew went back into the living room and sat down to talk to his Father about all that had happened and try to sort out a tangle of issues that would need his attention. He dug out the note from his son and found the section he had elected not to read to Andy. He took a deep breath and began to read.

> *Dad, knowing your perception, you're aware of the challenges you face with Margaret. This must hurt you deeply on top of everything else you're trying to work out. I didn't share my success with Margaret because I wanted her to accept me for who and what I was, not what I had. I knew her affection for me would be a lie if she knew my financial worth, and that would have been difficult for me to accept.*
>
> *I'm not sure what direction she will go, and my constant prayer was that she would not go to extremes to control the money. I've taken every legal precaution to ensure that Andy, through you, has control of my estate. Please contact Bob as soon as possible, and he will advise you if any portion of my will is challenged. Bob is a strong Christian and goes to God for guidance before every decision.*

Andrew thought, *You're right about one thing, son. This does hurt.* He reflected about how he knew Maggie had turned her back on the Lord but had no idea she had gone so far from his love. *What am I to do, Lord? It is hard to wait until someone does something before you can react. Damage control is so tricky because there is always the possibility that someone may be hurt. I can't let that someone be Andy. He has been hurt enough. Lord,*

Maggie knows the law, and I'm afraid she will use her knowledge to cause confusion. Even if she doesn't succeed, there are bound to be things said or done on both sides that will cause hurt and anger. Andrew remembered a passage that said, "I know, O Lord, that your laws are righteous, and in faithfulness you have afflicted me. May your unfailing love be my comfort, according to your promise to your servant. Let your compassion come to me that I may live, for your law is my delight"(Psalm 119:75–77).

Andrew sat there meditating on the words he had just prayed and reached for his Bible. Reading through the scripture, his eye rested on the words *your law.* He reread the passage several times and realized that God was telling him that His law took precedence over man's law. Each time brought him closer to shouting praise and adoration to his God and Father.

All Andrew could do was praise the God who knew all, understood the heart of man, and controlled every aspect of anything that would touch one of his own. Andrew continued laying all of his concerns at God's throne. *Lord, if there is something you can lead me to do that will spare Maggie shame, please keep me in a place where I will recognize what I should do or say. As a father, I would do whatever I can to spare my child pain, but Maggie is strong willed and, unfortunately, filled with pride and greed. I feel like David when he mourned losing his best friends, as Maggie once was to me. My beliefs and what I stand for are repulsive to her, Lord. I too am full of grief and can only call to you and spread out my hands, empty of solution, toward you to fill.*

Again Andrew waited on the Lord to feed his soul. After a short period of praise, heaviness was once again removed from his heart.

He knew that in the end he would be there to comfort his precious little Maggie, but not until she had gone through a fire that would leave a deep scar.

Chapter Nine

When Matt heard the car pull into the garage, he glanced at the clock on the mantel. Maggie walked into the kitchen and yelled for Matt. Matt walked into the kitchen and gave Maggie a big hug, saying, "Long day, sweetie?"

"You've got that right. I've had a lot of catching up to do since the funeral. Since it was so late, I stopped by and got Chinese takeout for supper."

"Great, we haven't had that in a long time."

"So how did your day go, hooky-player?" chided Maggie with a grin.

Matt went silent and thought about his conversation with Andrew that morning. Maggie looked up from the cartons she was opening. "Matt, what's wrong?"

Matt looked at Maggie, considering how much of the conversation with Andrew he would share with her. "Your dad called this morning and was going to see if you would pick him up at the airport at noon. He had lost track of time and forgot for a second that you would be at work. He decided to turn the rental car back in and use Harold's car while he's here. Anyway, I offered to pick him up, and we went for coffee before I took him back to Harold's house."

Matt had Margaret's full attention now. "What did you two talk about?"

"He wanted to know what I thought about the eulogy Andy gave his folks. He said he knew you didn't approve."

Margaret replied in a tone that was hostile and dripping with sarcasm. "And what was your answer?"

Matt was taken aback by her attitude; then he wondered why he would be surprised at her response as he answered, "I told him I was impressed with Andy's ability to speak in front of such a large crowd and that there was deep insight and knowledge in some of the things he said."

Matt's answer angered Margaret, and for a second she wondered why. She thought, *Matt is entitled to his opinion, and he didn't say he agreed with what was said, just that he was impressed.* Margaret's thoughts continued, *Yes, but that is the first step toward sympathizing with Andy and Andrew's faith and beliefs.* "Letting Andy speak to that crowd of people was garbage, and you know it, Matt! I think Andrew's lack of constraint on Andy's actions is an indication of his inability to raise Andy. Because of that and a few other things, I'm not sure that leaving Andy with Andrew is in Andy's best interest."

"What do you mean? What have you done?" Matt asked as his mind immediately went back to a warning Andrew had given him that morning.

"I'm looking into Andrew's financial stability. At his age, he won't be able to keep the farm much longer, even with Andy's help. If he's forced to sell the farm, where will he go? You know he can't take Andrew to an old folks' home. I just think it would be best if Andy didn't have to worry about making another major adjustment in his life until he at least finishes school."

At this point, Matt knew what was coming but asked, "So where do you think Andy needs to go, Margaret?"

Margaret wasn't ready to give Matt all the details yet. "Oh, I don't know. If nothing else he could live with us until he finishes high school. Then he could make his own decisions."

An alarm went off in Matt's mind. He knew there was more behind what was going on between Margaret and Andrew, but he also knew that Margaret wouldn't explain until she was ready. He decided to bring his side of the conversation to an end with, "Let's eat; I'm starving."

Margaret's mind wouldn't let her drop the topic that easily. There was something that told her to press Matt for more information about his talk with Andrew. "What else did you talk about this morning?"

"Your dad said he and Andy wouldn't be going back to Portland, at least for a while. With Andy's school, friends, church, and feeling secure at his folks' house, he thought it best to stay here. I don't think they will be leaving…at least until the estate is settled."

Matt's last statement caused Margaret to panic, and she forced herself to ask in a low, controlled voice, "Did he have anything else to say about Harold's estate?"

"No. Why? Margaret, what is going on? Your dad said he thought there could be trouble but wouldn't say when or why." The shocked look on Margaret's face confirmed that there was something going on, and he wasn't sure he really needed to know what it was.

Margaret didn't say anything, but her mind was racing with thoughts that she couldn't be totally responsible for. *Now what are you going to do? Andrew isn't going to lie down and play dead. He is going to fight you. How much does he know? Unless you want Andy's head to be filled with the junk your dad tried to force on you, you have to make sure Andrew doesn't have custody of Andy. Besides, Andrew is much too old to handle the kind of responsibility he'll need to control the kind of money Andy will inherit. You need to put a priority on getting Andy's guardianship moved into the courts and settled*. Matt called Margaret's name for the third time, and she lost her train of thought as she looked at him and said, "You're right. Let's eat."

● ● ● ● ● ● ● ● ● ● ● ● ● ● ● ● ●

Haphak was very nervous as he stood in Satan's chamber. His master was not happy about the events occurring in Andy's life. *Deadly silence is worse than the reprimands*, Haphak thought.

"You are wrong, Haphak," Satan countered, having heard Haphak's thoughts. "And you have no idea how far I *will* go with reprimands. But you *will* find out if you lose this soul."

Haphak was visibly shaken because he indeed did have an idea what happened when his master unleashed his full fury. He decided it was time to ask for help and stop trying to be the hero. "You know the adversary we are fighting is Andrew. He has a power that is impossible to penetrate, Master."

Satan's attitude softened toward Haphak because he did know about the hedge around Andrew, but his fury was ravenous as he saw this hedge being built around Andy. "Your strategy is influence, Haphak, not attack. Concentrate on who you can influence that in turn can use this same tactic against Andrew."

"You mean Margaret?"

"Yes, Margaret. Her greed has caused her to begin a strategy to control the boy. Guide her thoughts, Haphak."

Haphak left Satan and, with many helpers, immediately surrounded Margaret. Margaret and Matt had finished supper and were having iced tea on the patio. They were silent, each in deep thought. Margaret fantasized about having access to at least a million dollars and the things she could buy, including envy and admiration. *You've always wanted to be a trendsetter, and this is your chance. The old man is certainly not capable of raising another family at this point.* The idea of this thought certainly mirrored Margaret's desire but seemed to come from an outside source. *Oh well*, she thought, *they certainly are true. Dad is much too old to begin again, and the responsibility of counseling Andy about his money is beyond his capability.*

"What about inviting Dad and Andy over for dinner tomorrow night? We could barbecue steaks, and I'll pick up some sweet corn."

"Where did that come from, Margaret? I thought you said you wanted to keep as much distance between us and your dad as possible."

"Well, he is my dad, and after all, Andy did just lose his mom and dad. And his dad *was* my brother. Besides, I think it is time we got to know Andy. We haven't been a very good aunt and uncle to him."

"I think it's a great idea. It just surprises me that you do. However, since you're the executor of Harold's estate and Andrew mentioned he had stopped by the bank before I picked him up, you two probably have some things to talk about."

An alarm went off in Margaret's mind. "Did he say what he was doing at the bank?"

"No. Just that he was there longer than he had planned."

Did Bob tell him? You need to find out how much he knows as soon as possible. It could make a big difference in how you handle the hearing. "I think I'll give Dad a call and see if they have any plans for tomorrow night." Margaret's hands were sweating as she dialed Harold's phone number.

"Hello, Andrew speaking."

"Dad, is anything wrong? You sound tired."

"I am a bit. It's been a long day."

"Matt said you went to the bank and turned the car in today. I was wondering if you went to the bank because you needed money. If you need some spending money to hold you over, I could arrange that for you."

"No, Margaret. We have plenty." Andrew smiled as he answered Margaret's probe, knowing full well she was having a fit trying to find out if he knew Andy's financial worth.

"Oh. Well, did you see Mr. Clark?"

Good, Andrew thought, *she doesn't know how well I know Bob Clark.* "Yes, but he was just getting things started, so I didn't take up much of his time. Why? Do I need to talk to Mr. Clark?"

"Not really. I've met with him and have everything under control. Remember, if you need anything, just let *me* know, and I'll arrange it for you."

"I'll remember that, Maggie."

"Oh, by the way, I really called to see if you and Andy had any plans for dinner tomorrow evening. Matt and I thought we would barbecue some steaks out on the patio if you two could come over."

"That sounds great. I haven't had a good steak in a long time. Besides, we really haven't had a chance to sit down and talk yet. What time?"

"Come over about five thirty, and we'll plan to eat around six."

"Looking forward to it, Maggie."

* * * * * * * * * * * * * * * * * * *

Margaret decided to find out how Matt might feel about raising Andy. She wasn't sure how to open the conversation, so she skirted the issue with, "How do you feel about Andy, Matt?"

"I think he's a pretty neat kid, but unfortunately I don't know him very well."

"I suppose you blame me for that," Margaret said with a flare of temper.

"That's not what I said, and it's not what I was thinking. For heaven's sake, will you calm down? You've been climbing the wall ever since you got home."

Margaret thought about Matt's words for a second and realized she had overreacted to just about everything since she walked in the door. "I'm sorry, Matt. I'm just so stressed with everything." When Matt didn't answer, she heard, *Better play it cool, Margaret. You're going to need him on your side, and very soon, if everything goes according to plan. Let him think he has the lead for a while.* "I'm not sure what to do next."

Matt still did not answer but looked at Margaret's face for a clue about where she was really going, and he didn't like what he saw. Finally he said, "Margaret, don't you think it's time you told me what this is really all about? I know you well enough to know you have a plan in that pretty head of yours, and if you want my support, you need to tell me about it."

Now it was Margaret's turn to use silence and a stare to assess Matt's attitude. She didn't know whether to approach this head-on, skirt around it awhile longer, or just drop it for now. Since time was running out, she decided that Matt needed to be behind her in the fight she knew would come for custody of Andy. "Matt, Harold left Andy a lot of money. I don't think Dad is capable of being the administrator of Andy's finances or Andy, for that matter."

"How much money are we talking about?"

"Well over a million dollars," Margaret said matter-of-factly.

Matt was stunned into silence; then, just as bluntly, he stated, "So that's what all this is about. Does Andrew know?"

"I don't know. That's why I wanted to call him as soon as you said he had been to the bank today, but he didn't say anything about why he went to the bank when I spoke to him."

"You didn't exactly ask him, either."

"I'm not sure it's in my best interest right now to let him know I'm aware of the size of Andy's inheritance. What do you think?"

"I think the best approach is to be straightforward and honest with Dad and Andy. If they do know, Andrew might agree with you. But don't sell him short, Margaret. He's no dummy."

Margaret thought about this and added, "You're right. But I don't want to send the message that the money is the only thing I'm interested in. I also think it's important for Andy to experience areas of life other than the church so he knows his options and can make choices based on knowledge."

Matt sneered; he hadn't wanted to and immediately wished he had been more in control when Margaret said, "I can't believe this, Matt! You think it's only the money, don't you?"

"If I could answer that question on a scale of one to ten, I'd give it a pretty solid nine." They silently stared at one another; then Matt asked, "Are you going to deny it?"

"On your scale, I'd give it about a six. As I said before, I don't think Dad is capable of handling that kind of money. On the other hand, I do think Dad will try to manipulate Andy and his money by pressuring Andy with church, God, and the Bible. I think Andy needs to experience, or at least be exposed to, all this world has to offer. The eulogy he gave for Harold and Sarah almost sounded like a death wish. His head is so filled with the afterlife that he can't enjoy the life he has now."

Matt thought about the logic behind Margaret's statement. It sounded good, but he knew his wife and wondered if she really believed what she had just said.

Margaret was shocked at the statement she had just finished. *Where in the world did all that come from?* she thought. *It is all true, but to come up with all that out of the clear, blue sky…my, oh my, Margaret, you're better than you thought, and that's saying a lot.*

It was late. Standing up to end both the evening and the conversation, Matt headed for the patio door. "Let's wait until we get together tomorrow night and see where our conversation leads, Margaret."

Chapter Ten

Haphak was delighted with the lack of effort it took to influence what Margaret said and thought. The great news was that she was taking all the credit for her brilliance, and that was just fine…for a while. There was still a lot of work to be done. If Margaret was going to carry this off, she had to have Matt behind her, or she might be fighting more than one battle. Haphak knew that her focus had to be controlling Andy.

Margaret curled up on the comfortable padded lounge and enjoyed the cool evening breeze. She glanced at the moon fully reflected in the pool and wondered if she had told Andy to bring his bathing suit tomorrow. *Oh well. If he doesn't, he can borrow one of Matt's.* She continued with a smile, *As a matter of fact, there are many things we can give Andy.* The sky was clear and full of stars. For a fleeting second, the Creator of such beauty crossed her mind. *Get a grip on yourself, Margaret; you're starting to think like Harold.*

How did all of this come into being, Margaret?

Margaret jumped at the sudden audible interruption. "I thought you went to bed, Matt." Turning toward the patio door, she added, "What did you say?" An uneasy feeling engulfed Margaret as she saw no one behind her. *I did hear something. Some very weird things are going on.* She began a mental inventory of the last week of how many times she had given a spontaneous answer without really thinking them out. That was not at all like Margaret. As a lawyer, she had trained herself to not only think out her response but also to build scenarios of the different rebuttals to her statements. She also realized that hearing someone speak when no one was around seemed to be happening more frequently.

Nahal didn't like it, but he was held at a distance from Margaret. She had chosen her influence, and it wasn't the Spirit of the Almighty. Forces of evil surrounded her, and Haphak was calling the shots. Haphak shot a look that would kill, if possible, toward Nahal. Spinning around, he yelled, "Get back to your assignment and leave me to mine." Still looking directly into Nahal's eye, he whispered to Margaret, "What difference does it make? You aren't going to get sucked into all this religious stuff. There is a lot resting on tomorrow's dinner, and that is where my concentration needs to be." Margaret shook her head in agreement to her last thought, even though she wasn't sure where it came from. Haphak and Nahal knew where the thought had come from. To one, there was elation that Margaret's mind was becoming increasingly easier to control. To the other, there was a sadness that only heaven can understand.

* * * * * * * * * * * * * * * * * * *

Haphak was immediately in Satan's chamber. He, as always, was apprehensive about the master's mood. His success with Margaret should soften any castigation that he would have received a few days ago. *Silence and waiting to be recognized is always the hardest when I come here.*

"Feeling a little pleased with yourself, Haphak?"

He knew this was a lead-in but was not sure how he should respond. "I do feel like I've made some progress but came to get your advice and help, Master."

Satan sneered at Haphak's obvious attempt to placate his mood but knew that Haphak needed what he asked for. Suddenly and matter-of-factly, Satan replied, "You need help with Matt."

Not sure why he should be surprised that Satan would know this, Haphak simply shook his head and said, "Yes."

"You're very right, Haphak. Matt can be influenced because he is out of grace by being lukewarm." Satan knew how God felt about people who were neither for nor against him. "Be very careful, Haphak. Matt is not convinced that Margaret is entirely wrong. On the other hand, if he is too exuberant in his support, Margaret may suspect that something's not quite right."

"How should I approach him?"

"With a dream. He is asleep, and the conversation he and Margaret had tonight is still fresh."

Haphak knew the interview was over. He was immediately next to Matt's sleeping body. *How should I influence this being? Greed isn't Matt's weakness. How about jeopardizing his marriage and home? No. He might come on too strong. Ah! I know, the Good Samaritan. He can save Andy by being a father image and friend.*

Matt shifted his position and entered a deep sleep. He saw himself and Andy laughing and talking while they walked toward the ticket booth at Safeco Field to take in a ballgame. He heard Andy remark, "This is great, Uncle Matt! I haven't been to a ballgame since Dad died. Papa doesn't think about ballgames. Guess it's because he was always so busy on the farm he never had time."

"What do you and Andrew do for fun, Andy?"

"Read the Bible and talk about God, mostly. There's also a lot of stuff going on at the church, so we spend a lot of time there."

"Is that fun for you?"

"Yeah, I enjoy it. I also love being with Papa and remembering times that Dad and I did things at the church. It would be nice, though, if we could go fishing or go to a ballgame once in a while."

"Well, how about you and me putting a fishing trip together for next weekend? We could even ask Andrew to join us, if you like."

"You mean it? That would be great, Uncle Matt."

Haphak had accomplished his mission with Matt, so he returned to Margaret, who was just giving the doors and alarm system a final check before retiring for the night. He wondered if he shouldn't give Margaret a little dream push. *What could it hurt?* he thought and waited for her to enter into a deep sleep.

Margaret saw herself sitting in a plush office facing an older gentleman sitting behind a large, mahogany desk. "What can this school offer my nephew, Mr. Markson?"

"We feel young men should explore as many options as possible, Mrs. Selby. Art, the classics, world history and how it affects today's world, government, and finances."

"What about religion? Andy has had extensive, strict religious training."

"Ah yes, religion! We feel it's beneficial for our young men to understand the cultures and origins of major religions around the world. If Andy leans toward Christianity, doesn't the Bible mention the fact that God's Spirit will fill men with skill, ability, and knowledge in all kinds of things?"

"Excellent. Andy's ability to make educated decisions for his life has been hampered by being taught a very narrow viewpoint." The scenery shifted, and Margaret was now standing at the head of an oval table, instructing her staff of ten professional men and women. She felt the elation of self-confidence and unchallenged power. So powerful was the feeling that she woke up with an obsessive need to plan her strategy to make it happen. She began by thinking about all the benefits she could offer everyone involved. *Dad could go back to his precious farm and not be bothered by having to raise another family. Andy would have the benefit of a well-rounded education that would certainly broaden his choices based on knowledge. And Matt and I could…well, that's another matter,* she thought with an audible laugh.

●　●　●　●　●　●　●　●　●　●　●　●　●　●　●　●　●

Andrew looked at the clock beside his bed. *Two thirty and I'm still awake. What's going on, Lord?* He got up, grabbed his robe, and went to the kitchen for a cup of tea. He quietly waited on the Lord to speak to his heart. Andrew quickly realized the problem; Maggie was in trouble. *How do I pray for her, Lord? Maggie lives only for the bread of this world and doesn't realize that it will not sustain her. There will always be the need for more, and the hunger will never be satisfied. She knows that you are the only bread that will appease her hunger, but as you said, she was told but does not choose to believe.*

Maggie's heart is being filled with evil, Lord, so I pray in Jesus's name that you send your warriors to fight the forces that are trying to destroy my daughter.

The very familiar, still voice answered, *Andy is in my hand. He is secure in my plans for his life. Trust him, Andrew, for he will be the instrument of influence in the life of your daughter. Margaret battles with the conflict of things she lusts for in the world and the things she was taught as a child. Have I not said that if you train a child in the way he should go that when he is old he will not turn from it (Proverbs 22:6)?*

Andrew felt the peace of a small child when there was the confidence that Dad would take care of everything.

Chapter Eleven

The following day was quiet, and Andrew was thankful. He had taken the papers back to the bank and felt at peace about having that done. At three thirty, Andy ran in the front door and headed for the refrigerator. He grabbed the carton of orange juice and took a quick gulp. Andrew walked into the kitchen and asked, "Hey, tell me about your day at school. How was it? Were your friends glad when you told them you weren't moving?"

Andy sat down at the kitchen table and answered in a low voice, "Yeah, they were all glad I wasn't moving, but everyone brought up Mom and Dad, and I started crying. It was real embarrassing, but I just couldn't help it. I really thought I had gotten past that, but I guess it's going to take a little more time. There were a couple of new kids, though, Larry and Laura. They're twins, and Laura is someone I hope to know better."

Andrew's heart went out to Andy; he had expected this would happen when Andy said he wanted to go to school the day before. Andrew put his hand on Andy's shoulder as he thought, *The good news is that it is Friday and there will be two days for Andy to forget today. It's also a good thing that there is only one more week of this school year left.* "Andy, these things work themselves out differently in everyone. For some, it is a hurt that's buried deep, and the hurt may not surface for a long time. For others, the mourning is like a bursting dam that floods, and then it's over. For most, though, the hurt is worked out a little at a time, as the good Lord knows we are ready to handle it. Take heart, son. If the Father knew you weren't ready to handle today, something would have come up to prevent you from going."

"He really cares that much, Papa?"

"More than you could ever know. He knows more about you than you do."

"How could he know me better than I know myself?"

"Well, answer me this, Andy: how many hairs do you have on your head?"

"Nobody could answer that question."

"God can! In Matthew ten, he's talking about how precious you are to him."

Andy ran to get his dad's Bible and turned to Matthew 10. "Where is it, Papa?"

"Look at verses twenty-nine and thirty."

Andy read the passages and closed the Bible. "Wow, that's pretty awesome, huh, Papa?"

"You bet it is."

Andy changed the subject. "Do you think we should talk about the money at Aunt Margaret's tonight?"

"Do you think we should?"

"Not really. I'm not too comfortable with the whole idea yet. I'm not even sure if I'm happy about it. That doesn't make sense, does it? Who in their right mind wouldn't be happy about that kind of money?"

"People who have the mind of God. You don't need money or possessions to find your joy. In righteousness is where you'll find true wealth. Let's take a lesson from Harold and see what God has to say about it. I think it's time you come to grips with your inheritance.

Your saying that you're not sure how you feel about wealth is really very encouraging, but the fact is you are wealthy. Now let's see what God thinks about it."

"That will help a lot. Dad and I always settled things by going to God's Word." Andy picked up the Bible again. "So where do I start?"

Andrew laughed at Andy's enthusiasm and also understood that continuing the tradition that Andy and Harold started helped after the day he had at school. "Well, God said that 'Wealth is worthless in the day of wrath, but righteousness delivers from death'" (Proverbs 11:4).

Andrew gave Andy a second to digest what he had said then added, "Proverbs 11:28 says, 'Whoever trusts in his riches will fall, but the righteous will thrive like a green leaf.' From just these two scriptures, we see that when you're in trouble, money isn't going to solve your problem. You've heard the saying, 'Money can't buy happiness.' But the righteous man knows that turning to God in times of need will solve his problems. A green leaf is full of life, Andy. It can bend in a wind and take the beating of the sun and rain and continue to thrive. This money is an inheritance from your father, and I know that if he hadn't been satisfied that you had a good foundation in the Lord and the wisdom that we read about in Ecclesiastes seven, verses eleven and twelve, Harold would have made other plans for you."

Andy scrambled to find Ecclesiastes 7 and found verses 11 and 12. "It says that an inheritance is a good thing here. God says it's like wisdom, but the difference is that wisdom preserves life. What does that mean?"

"Well, Proverbs three is talking about wisdom. It calls wisdom a 'her,' and we're told that her ways are pleasant ways and all her paths are peace. It goes on to say that she is a tree of life to those who embrace her, and those who lay hold of her will be blessed. You see, Andy, God is saying that there is nothing wrong with being wealthy. As a matter of fact, he gives wealth. Look at Job and Abraham. Even after he took everything away from Job, in the end, he restored Job's possessions."

Andy was considering all his grandfather had said when Andrew added, "Now let's look at another side of wealth. You know there are people who want the things rich people have so bad that they act like they are rich. Old folks call it "putting on the dog." Andrew said this with a chuckle. "The same verse talks about people who really do have wealth but don't act like it. Let me put it another way: if you really are rich, you don't need to prove anything. We're given a warning about riches in Mark chapter four, verses eighteen and nineteen. Even people who know the Lord can get caught up in the love of money and the things it can do here on earth. Read these verses when you get a chance, and we can talk about it later if you want to. Just remember, if you are rich in righteousness, God's Word, and depend on his blessing, you have greater wealth than money could ever give you."

"I think I understand, but I'll need some time, you've given me a lot to think about."

Andy grabbed his dad's Bible and started into the living room. Just before he reached the door to leave, Andrew said, "Don't go far. We need to leave for Margaret's in about an hour.

Chapter Twelve

Margaret fought the irritation that had become normal for her when she knew she had to spend time with her father. *Get it together, Margaret. Tonight is too important for you to mess it up with your mood. Be on your best behavior; you need to know what Andrew knows, and you need to know now.*

Matt interrupted Margaret's thoughts. "Did you put the steaks in a marinade?"

"I put them in the sauce this morning before I went to work. Are the coals ready? Dad and Andy should be here any time. I told them five thirty, and it's a quarter to six, so you may as well get them started." Margaret went to the refrigerator and took the steaks out to Matt. "I'm so glad it's a warm evening; we can spend most of the time visiting with Dad by the pool, and Andy can swim if he wants to."

"I bet that conversation will be an interesting one."

"What's that suppose to mean? I just want a chance to make sure everything is going okay with those two and find out if there is anything I can do for…" Margaret heard the doorbell and thought, *Saved by the bell.* She could feel Matt's eyes on her back as she walked to the side of the house to holler for her dad and Andy to come around back.

Andrew raised his nose in the air, took a deep sniff, and said, "Boy, you can smell those steaks clear around to the front. What kind of sauce is that?"

"It's a special marinade we found in England last year. Matt added his special touch, and believe me, it tastes as good as it smells."

Margaret opened her arms to her father, and returning her embrace, Andrew prayed for the day he could walk into her heart. He could feel his daughter's resistance and was looking forward to what this evening would bring.

Walking toward the grill, Margaret asked, "How have you two been doing? We've talked on the phone, but I haven't had time to really visit with you since the funeral."

Before Andy or Andrew could answer, Matt approached Andrew with his hand extended and said, "Welcome, Andrew. We put this off for much too long." He ruffled Andy's hair and asked, "How do you like your steak, tiger?"

"Medium rare, Uncle Matt. Boy, am I hungry!"

"Great! My cooking always tastes better when people are hungry enough to eat anything," Matt answered with a grin.

"Go ahead and grab a plate, salad, and potato. I'll get the lemonade, and we can eat." Margaret carried the tray of drinks to the table and dreaded what she knew had to happen. But with a sigh of resolve, she said, "Would you like to say grace, Dad?"

Andrew inwardly grinned at how hard that had to be for his daughter but answered, "Sure." Everyone bowed their heads, and Andrew decided to make his request to the Lord short but sincere. "Lord, bless this food. Bless this house and all present. Thank you for your Son and grace. In Jesus's name, amen."

Margaret couldn't believe her luck. They filled their plates and were too busy eating to hold a meaningful conversation.

Matt cleared his throat and looking at Andy said, "You know, it's early, but we've had a mild spring, and other than it being a bit frosty in the mornings, it's been pretty decent weather. How would you two like to go camping and catch a few fish up in the Blue Mountains next weekend?"

"Wow, Uncle Matt! That would be great. How about it, Papa? Doesn't that sound like a good idea?"

Andrew smiled at his grandson and at the same time realized that he hadn't thought about the things he knew seventeen-year-old boys liked and needed to do. He wrinkled his brow and looked at Margaret with his answer. "You know, since we've decided to stay a while longer, I really need to make a quick trip to the farm and make sure everything is okay. There are a few business matters I need to take care of too." Looking back at Andy, he continued, "I think a fishing trip is the best idea I've heard in a long time, Andy. Matt and Margaret, would you object if Andy spent a couple of days with you after next weekend? If I leave next Friday, I could be back Tuesday or Wednesday."

Margaret was stunned; she couldn't believe she just heard what she knew Andrew had just said. What an opportunity to start a very important bonding process with Andy. "Are you kidding, Dad? We would love it. I'll even try to take off an extra day for the weekend."

Matt was also a little surprised at Andrew's suggestion and asked Andy, "How does that sound to you, Andy?"

Andy hesitated a bit too long and stared at his grandfather. "It really sounds like a lot of fun, Uncle Matt, but I really think I need to be with Papa in case he needs me."

For the first time since Andrew arrived, he realized that in Andy's mind, the support role had been reversed, and Andy felt obligated to take care of him. "Andy, I'll be fine. There's a lot of running I need to do, and as soon as I get things taken care of, I'll be back. I really think it makes a lot more sense for you to go camping next weekend and enjoy Matt and Margaret's pool. Don't you?"

Andy said, "I guess so," but his displeasure was apparent.

Margaret stood up, stacked the empty plates, and announced that dessert was on the way. She walked into the kitchen, sat the plates in the sink, and wondered about divine intervention. *For someone who depends on God, his God just let Andrew make a huge mistake. Or if God really is running this show, he must realize that Andrew is not capable of making the decisions that will be necessary to manage the future of a very wealthy young man.*

* * * * * * * * * * * * * * * * * * * *

Wednesday was the last day of school. Andy had settled back into his circle of friends from church and daily routine, but now that school was over, he wondered what he would do with his summer. Summer was a time he had always looked forward to, mainly because of his dad. They always found time for weekend getaways, building something in the garage, or just hanging out together.

Thinking about the upcoming fishing trip reminded him of a weekend he and his dad spent in the mountains two years ago. They left home at about three one Friday afternoon and drove to their favorite camping site in the Blue Mountains. It took very little time to set up camp, start a fire, and try to catch a trout for dinner. Andy gave a small snort when he remembered how many times he and his dad had settled for peanut butter and crackers the first night. The following morning, he woke up early and decided not to wake Harold. *Wouldn't it be a feather in my cap if I caught breakfast and had it cooked before Dad woke up?* he remembered thinking that morning. Grabbing his pole and wading boots, he started walking up the stream. Time flew by as Andy walked farther and farther upstream, concentrating on the next cast. The sun was warm on his back, and looking up, he realized it was later than he thought. *I'll just cast out ten more times and take five more steps*, he thought, *then head back*. He saw a spot just ahead. He started toward the pool when he heard, "Having any luck, young man?"

"Not really," Andy yelled without turning around. He thought he should be friendly and talk to the stranger, and yelling probably scared the fish anyway, so he reeled in his line and started for the bank that was four or five steps away. Taking the third step, he heard a loud, cracking sound. He spun around just in time to see a large limb break off and crash into the stream right where he had been standing two seconds earlier. Hurrying to the bank, he started to thank the stranger for calling out to him, but no one was there. He looked up and down the stream and into the trees but could see no one. He even yelled, "Hey, mister!" a couple of times but received no answer. It took ten minutes to get back to camp, and Andy thought about the incident all the way. He told Harold what had happened and was surprised when his dad told him that about a half an hour ago he had felt an urgent need to pray for his son. Harold never questioned God. When he was told to pray, he prayed.

Andy came back to the present and thought, *I'd better be careful next weekend with Uncle Matt. I don't think he has the same connections my dad had.*

• • • • • • • • • • • • • • • • • •

The drive to the campsite on the Tucanan River brought back fond memories for Andy. It hadn't been that long since Andy and his folks had made the trip, and each familiar landmark reminded him of songs they sang and conversations they had on that trip. Andy wondered if his family would have done anything differently had they known it would be the last camping trip they would have as a family.

Matt saw Andy's expression in the rearview mirror and somehow knew what was going through Andy's mind.

"How ya doing back there, Andy?"

"Okay. It just seems kinda sad remembering the last time I took this trip."

"Yeah, I know. But hang in there, buddy. It just takes time."

Margaret thought this would be the right time to change the mood by telling Matt and Andy her surprise.

"I have a special treat for you, Andy."

"Really? What?"

"Well, I spoke to your school principal last week, and he said your academic success was outstanding. He said it was difficult for the school to challenge you and you probably couldn't reach your full potential in that school."

"Wow! The principal said that?"

Margaret was pleased that Andy seemed anxious to hear more. She continued, "So I've been looking around to see if there was a school that could take you further than your school. I think I found an excellent school that will open up doors you never dreamed possible."

Andy wasn't sure he liked where this was going, but he didn't want to hurt Margaret's feelings, so he asked, "Where is this school, Aunt Margaret?"

"Actually, it's here in the Blue Mountains, not far from where we'll camp. If you're interested, I set up an appointment for you to see the school tomorrow. How does that sound?" Margaret thought Andy was quiet a bit too long and added, "We don't have to go if you don't want to. I'll call the school and let them know that you didn't want to visit."

Matt thought Margaret's last words were unnecessary and gave her a look that let her know it. Margaret looked at Matt, raised her eyebrows, and shrugged as if to say, "Who cares what you think!"

Andy didn't know what to do. On one hand, he really wasn't interested in seeing or having anything to do with another school. But on the other hand, he didn't want his aunt to think he didn't appreciate all the trouble she had gone to for his benefit. After a long pause, Andy said, "I guess it wouldn't hurt to see the school, but I hate to cut our camping trip short. It's been a long time since I was camping and fishing, and I may not get another chance for a while."

Matt had bought a tent large enough for ten people, but putting it up was fast and easy. Andy had a pup tent. Margaret unloaded the cooking utensils, her cot, and the sleeping bags. Matt started a fire with some dry wood he had thrown in the back of the truck, and Andy ran into the woods to gather wood for a stockpile. Matt grabbed a five-gallon water bucket and filled a large pot. He had a grate over the fire, and putting the pot on the grate, he yelled, "Hey, Andy! How about seeing if we can catch our dinner for tonight? We can give some worms a swimming lesson while Margaret boils some macaroni, just in case."

"You bet, Uncle Matt. I've already got my pole ready to go."

Matt and Andy walked upriver a couple hundred yards, baited their hooks, and sat down to wait.

"It didn't strike me that you were thrilled about a new school, Andy," Matt said. Andy wasn't sure how to respond to Matt's statement but decided the best thing to do was be open and honest.

"You know, Uncle Matt, I don't want you or Aunt Margaret to think I'm not grateful that you're trying to look out for my best interest, but I don't even want to think about a new school right now."

"Whoa, buddy! This school thing was as big a surprise to me as it was for you. I heard about it for the first time today, the same time you did."

"I'm not sure what this is all about, Uncle Matt. Papa would have said something to me if he knew about it. Why would Aunt Margaret look into something like this without talking to me or Papa about it?"

Matt was sure he knew the answer but said nothing to Andy. He was relieved when his pole started dragging down. "Hey, I got first bite. Now watch me land this baby."

Andy was excited for Matt and started giving him the automatic advice one always hears when trying to reel in a fish when his line started unwinding. Andy gave a quick jerk and started slowing, reeling the line back in. Before long, two nice-sized trout were lying in the grass, and nothing else was as important as getting their lines back into the stream.

Andy was having a great time with his uncle, but he couldn't help thinking about the last time he and his dad had been here competing for the biggest catch. Matt noticed the expression on Andy's face and asked, "Thinking about your dad?"

"Yeah. He always took whatever time he needed to make me feel important. Isn't it funny how we don't think about those things until it's too late to let the person know how much you appreciate what they did? Guess with that being said, thanks for taking the time for this trip."

"I can't remember how long it's been since I came up here to camp and fish. It's a real treat for me too. Andy, I'm really sorry that I didn't know you and Harold better, but I hope you and I can become good friends."

"Me too."

Margaret watched the fire jump around the wood in the fire pit. *How like people the fire is, randomly jumping up to gain the best advantage wherever there is an opening or opportunity. What they fail to understand is that without the hot coals at the base of the fire, the fire would go out. In the meantime, the flames jump up only to burn themselves out as they hungrily eat the fuel. I'm content for now to be the source. If Andy isn't ready to fall into line with my plans, I'll go to plan B. The only problem I'll have is the old man, getting him to agree that a home with Matt and me would be best for Andy.*

"Hey, Aunt Margaret! Hope you didn't put on that macaroni. Look what we caught."

Margaret had forgotten all about the task she had been given. "Are you kidding? I had every confidence we would eat fish for dinner."

Matt cleaned the fish while Andy peeled potatoes and Margaret made a salad. Andy said, "Cooking over an open fire is my specialty."

With a wave of his arm to his middle and a low bow, he added, "So allow me." He diced the potatoes into a hot skillet and added the fish to another skillet that had a couple of pieces of sizzling bacon. Dinner was soon ready to eat, and they had all worked up an appetite.

"Do you mind if I bless the food?" Andy asked.

Margaret rolled her eyes and thought, *Boy, do they have this kid brainwashed! Even out here he can't relax.*

Matt answered, "Sounds like a great idea, Andy," and bowed his head.

"Thanks for the food, Father. Thanks for this trip. Thank you for Uncle Matt and Aunt Margaret. Bless the food…and by the way, thanks for the fish. Amen."

Matt grinned at Andy as he added his *amen* and, grabbing a paper plate, announced, "Let's eat."

"You pray like you talk, Andy. I've noticed you don't use a lot of *thees* and *thous*."

"Dad taught me how to pray, Aunt Margaret. He told me that God was my heavenly Father and I should talk to him with simplicity and truth. Hey, you might as well; you can't hide anything from him anyway. He already knows what we're going to do or say before we even think about it."

This thought bothered Margaret, but she quickly shrugged it off. "You think about God and church a lot, don't you, Andy?"

"Yes, I do. But how can you help it? Look up. When I look up into the sky on a night like this, 'The heavens declare the glory of God; the skies proclaim the work of his hands' (Psalm 19:1). How can you look at a night sky like that and not think about God?"

"How can you remember verses in the Bible so well that you can just pull one out of your hat at any time, Andy? That's amazing. It just proves my point about your intelligence and need for a better education." Her thoughts continued with, *And a broader outlook on life. I can't fault you for your outlook on life. You remind me so much of Harold when we were close. One thing I can say about Harold and you too is you are kind. But you need to know that life can offer you a lot more than church and God.*

"All the credit goes to my dad. He and I spent hours memorizing scriptures. He said you never knew when you would need a verse to explain something."

Matt knew where this conversation was going, so he said, "Hey, the fish bite early, sport. We'd better hit the hay so we have an advantage tomorrow."

"Right. I really had a blast today. Thank you both." Andy headed for his little tent but turned just before going in and said, "I love you, guys. Good night."

"Thanks, sport! That was a real nice thing to say," Matt answered.

Margaret was a bit surprised when she realized her normal response was *Love you too* but didn't say anything. Instead, she heard herself asking Matt, "What was that all about?"

Matt looked at Margaret with a look of half disbelief and half disgust. "What's gotten into you? You question everything, and you're defensive about any answer you get."

"I am not! You know, your holier-than-thou attitude is getting a bit tiresome. Grow up, Matt. The world isn't as rosy as you seem to think it is."

"No good will come from continuing this conversation. I'm going to bed. Do you want me to put out the fire, or do you want to do it?"

"I'll do it. Go on to bed and bury your head under the covers."

As Matt retreated toward the tent, he said, "For Pete's sake, Margaret! Loosen up! I'm not the enemy here."

Matt's last statement lingered on Margaret's mind. *Who is the enemy? On one hand, things aren't going as smoothly as I want them to. But on the other hand, when the stakes are this high, why would I think it would be easy? It's all this religion stuff—that's the enemy. If Harold had raised Andy like a normal kid, he wouldn't have a problem accepting some of the fun things kids do. What normal kid thinks that going to church seven days a week is fun?*

I'll bet he's never even tried to kiss a girl. Harold really did Andy an injustice by sheltering him from everything except God. Well, I'm going to have to change that, and this school is the ticket for Andy. It may take some doing, but we are going to stop on our way home.

Andy lay in his tent and thought about how exciting it was to catch a fish again. It had been a long time since he and his dad had taken a day to fish. Andy's thoughts turned toward prayer as he thought about the school Margaret wanted him to see. *What should I do, Lord? I guess it's up to me at this point whether I agree to check it out or not. Do you get involved in something this simple? It would just be easier if I knew if this was something you wanted or something Aunt Margaret wants so she doesn't have to feel obligated to me because she's my aunt. Oh well. Guess this is one of those things that Dad and Papa meant when they said, "Trust in the* Lord *with all your heart and lean not on your own understanding; in all your ways acknowledge him, and he will make your paths straight."*

Andy fell into a restful sleep before he could finish praying. He saw himself walking along the stream where he and Matt had fished that day. The path turned toward the water. The gentle stream was now a raging river moving so fast it looked as if the water and rocks were having a battle. The water rushed over the rocks, attempting to move them, and the rocks remained steadfast, refusing to budge. Andy turned to go back the way he had come, but the path was not there. Now there were rock walls on three sides and the river in front of him. He heard himself repeating the scripture about trusting the Lord but adding, "But there is no path, Lord. I don't know what to do. Please help me."

Suddenly he looked up the river and saw where a log bridged the river. Andy ran to the log, but when he tried to stand on it, the log rolled. Andy caught himself by grabbing the branch of a tree hanging over the log. He felt helpless and again heard himself asking, "Why would you put a log here that wasn't safe, Lord? I trusted you to show me a way of escape, but taking that way out would have killed me."

Andy felt safe again as he saw himself sitting at the kitchen table with his grandpa. "Why would God tell me to trust him but then put me in danger, Papa?"

"You only paid attention to the part of the scripture that you thought was important, Andy."

"I don't know what you mean. I needed a way out, and God's Word said, 'Trust in the Lord.' That's what I did, and it really wasn't a way out."

"Ah. Yes, Andy! It does say, 'Trust in the Lord with all your heart,' but it also says, 'Lean not on your own understanding,' and, 'in all your ways acknowledge Him.' You saw the log and reasoned that the log bridge was your way out, right?"

"Well, sure. Actually, it was the only way out. There were only cliffs on the other sides."

"What did you think when you saw the log?"

"I thought that because I had thought about what the Bible said about trusting God that he must have put the log there for me to walk across."

"Right. And did you stop and consider any other options? Look around a little? Ask God if that was the way? Or just jumped for the first escape route you saw? The Father does give us a way out, but he also gave us a mind and will. He wants us to consider the options, not jump at the first door that opens. What I'm saying is that your understanding told you that the log was the only way out. Instead of jumping on the log, you should have thought about that part of the scripture that says, 'In all your ways acknowledge him.' Did you ask if that was the way or even thank him for providing the bridge?"

"No!" Andy answered, feeling embarrassed.

Andrew chuckled as he patted Andy on the shoulder and said, "Wish I had a penny for every time I've been caught leaning on my own understanding. I'd be richer than you are."

Andy looked up in surprise. "Really?"

"Really. I don't know of anyone who isn't guilty of that one. It is an easy one to do because God did give us a brain and he meant for us to use it. But when we are faced with a dangerous decision or one that could change our whole future, we need to acknowledge him and wait for him to keep his word and straighten the path. Now you go back to that river and try again."

Andy started to protest as he was faced with the log and river on one side and rock walls on the others. It was the last place he wanted to be. Before he could say *Maybe some other time*, he was again standing on the riverbank, looking at the log.

Remembering what Andrew had said, Andy sat down and started to talk to his heavenly Father. *God, if you put the log here for me to cross over, then thank you, and I'll trust you to make it safe. If there is something else you want me to see, then please show it to me.* Andy tried to be quiet like his papa did when he waited on the Lord for guidance, but his papa's words kept intruding. He'd said, "Did you look around?" Andy realized the size of the rocks that walled him in and the fierce river were so overwhelming that he hadn't taken time to look around. He stood on the bank of the river and looked westerly across the river. He made a quarter turn and faced south, the direction he came from, and slowly circled around to the east, seeing only rock. He continued turning and was stunned when he saw a narrow path that continued skirting the riverbank. But it looked like it disappeared into the river. Andy decided to check it out. He went a few feet and saw that the path only looked like it went into the river. A rock had rolled across the path at a narrow point, and from where Andy was at the log, it looked like the path ended. The path turned abruptly and lay wide and straight on into a valley. He heard his grandfather say, *You must never just take the part you want from God's Word, Andy. Consider all his words.*

Andy woke up to the sound of a crackling fire. It was cold in his little tent, and he quickly threw on his jeans, sweatshirt, shoes, and coat. Crawling out of his tent, he saw his uncle Matt putting a pan of water on the fire grate.

"Morning, Uncle Matt."

"Hey, sport. Did you sleep good?"

"Yeah. But right now I just want to get as close to that fire as I can," Andy answered with a little chuckle.

Andy and Matt were silent for a few minutes as Andy warmed by the fire. Margaret joined them and said, "I had no idea it was this chilly up here in the morning. Did you sleep well, Andy?"

"Sure did, Aunt Margaret."

"Did you think about stopping at the school for a look?"

"Sure, Aunt Margaret. It's okay with me if we stop."

"Great. I think you'll be surprised. If we are going to stop, we should leave here no later than noon, Matt."

"Sounds good. That will give me and Andy a couple hours to get some more worms wet."

After eating a breakfast of sausage and pancakes, Matt and Andy were on their way back to the river. "Are you sure you don't mind stopping at the school, Andy?"

"You know, Uncle Matt, the way I see it, looking isn't going to hurt anything. But I only have one more year at school, and I want to graduate with my class. I've gone clear through school with some of those kids and have some really great friends."

Matt just shook his head in agreement with Andy's logic.

At eleven thirty, they were throwing the last of their camping gear in the truck, and after throwing one more shovel of dirt on the fire, they were on their way. About an hour later, they sat in front of an iron gate, and Margaret picked up a phone mounted on a rock post. A young voice answered the ring. "Welcome to Cascade Academy. How may I help you?"

"My name is Margaret Selby. I believe the president is expecting us. My secretary called last week and set up an appointment."

After a brief silence, the young man was back on the phone and said, "Yes, Mrs. Selby. Dr. Frum is expecting you."

The gate slowly opened, and they drove to the front of a white building that looked like a mansion complete with three-story columns that extended the full length of the front of the building.

Dr. Frum waited for them at the building entrance. He looked like he was in his late fifties, had slightly gray hair, and was thirty pounds overweight. Margaret led the group as they approached Dr. Frum. Extending his hand, he introduced himself as the principal of Cascade Academy. "I'm so glad you were able to make it, Mrs. Selby. Your secretary said you would call if your plans changed."

Margaret didn't know why, but she was a bit embarrassed that Andy had heard that last remark. Margaret decided to shrug it off by stating, "Thank you, Dr. Frum. Our visit was really up to my nephew here, Andy Staple."

Andy stepped around his aunt and extended his hand to Dr. Frum. "Let's go to my office, have some refreshments, and talk before we take a tour of the school."

As they entered Dr. Frum's office, Margaret let out a gasp that caught the attention of everyone in the group. "Is everything okay, Margaret?" Matt asked.

Margaret tried to sound like she had heard something funny. "I'm fine, Matt. It's just one of those déjà vu things. I know I've never been here, but this room looks so familiar." Margaret was not okay. It was the same plush office and mahogany desk she had seen in her dream. As a matter of fact, the only difference between Dr. Frum and the man in her dream was the name.

Dr. Frum directed his questions to Andy. "Why were you interested in seeing our school, Andy?"

The question caught Andy off guard, and he wasn't sure how to answer the question truthfully without sounding disrespectful to his aunt. "Aunt Margaret said she had heard a lot of good things about your school, Dr. Frum. Since we were in the area, we thought it was a good idea to tour the school."

Looking at Margaret, Dr. Frum arched one eyebrow, indicating an unspoken question of why. Margaret caught the look and said, "You know, Andy, I'll bet it would be a lot more fun for you if one of Dr. Frum's cadets gave you a tour."

"I'd like that, if it's all right with you, Dr. Frum."

"Absolutely," Dr. Frum stated as he walked to his desk and pushed a buzzer. A young man entered the room. "What can I do for you, Doctor?"

"Would you mind giving this young lad a tour of the academy, John?"

"Not at all," John answered.

"Oh!" Dr. Frum said. "This is John Staats, my assistant." Matt stood and took John's extended hand. Margaret remained seated but offered her hand in greeting. "John has been here at Cascade for the past ten months. He has fulfilled his student field training as my assistant, and I have to say, if there was any way I could convince him to stay, I would."

"Thank you, Dr. Frum," John responded with a smile. "It has been an interesting year. Shall we go, Andy?"

Andy and John went out a back door that opened up to a panorama of modern buildings, each landscaped with benches, trees, and grass that rivaled a park. "Wow," Andy said.

John chuckled. "I know what you mean, Andy. It really is a beautiful campus."

They walked along a path while John pointed out the purpose each building served. He turned onto another path leading into what appeared to be a dense forest. "It looks like the path disappears, John." Andy's remark sounded more like a question than a statement.

"Yes, it does. This path leads to the area where the boys live. It's designed this way so that there is a separation between school and home. We don't want the boys to feel like they are in school all the time. Why do you think this school is the place for you?"

Andy decided to tell John the truth. "It's really not my idea. Aunt Margaret thinks I need exposure to things other than my church involvement, I think."

"I see." John stopped and looked at Andy. "So what are your plans?"

"Honestly, I plan to finish my senior year at my old school and then go to seminary."

John smiled down at Andy. "I think that is a great plan."

Andy relaxed a little. "Dr. Frum said you were leaving here. Where are you going?"

"I have an appointment with the First Baptist Church in Pasco as their youth minister. Are you familiar with that church?"

Andy laughed. "Hey, that's great. That's my church, and it's a really good church with lots of teens."

"I'm looking forward to working with you."

Andy and John made their way back to the administration building and found Margaret, Matt, and Dr. Frum standing on the porch saying their good-byes.

"There you are," Margaret greeted. "What do you think of the campus, Andy?"

"It's really cool. Most of it looks like a park."

Margaret extended her hand to Dr. Frum and said, "Thank you again for seeing us, Dr. Frum. We will let you know our decision soon."

Margaret, Matt, and Andy were soon in the car, driving out the main gate. There was an anxious silence in the car. Matt broke the silence. "So do you think you will consider attending the academy?"

Margaret glared at Matt. She had worked out a plan on how to approach Andy about attending the school, and Matt had just ruined everything.

"I don't think it's right for me, Uncle Matt, but I did learn one piece of exciting news."

"Oh?" Margaret said as she turned to face Andy. "And what was that?"

"John is going to be our youth pastor next year. Isn't that great?"

Margaret sat in stunned silence. *Maybe that school wasn't the best choice for Andy after all. A place that turns out youth pastors isn't what I had in mind.*

Andy continued with, "Are you really disappointed in my decision, Aunt Margaret?"

Margaret was deep in thought about her alternatives and didn't answer. Andy misunderstood Margaret's silence for anger and said nothing more. Matt looked at Margaret and said, "Margaret, did you hear Andy?"

"What…what did you say, Matt?"

"Did you hear Andy ask if you were disappointed with his decision?"

"Oh! No, Andy, of course not. You are old enough to know what's best for you."

Andy was relieved; he had really enjoyed spending the weekend with his aunt and uncle and wanted to continue a relationship with them. *After all,* he thought, *other than Papa, they are the only family I have left.*

• • • • • • • • • • • • • • • • • •

On Tuesday afternoon, Matt, Margaret, and Andy pulled into the driveway and saw Harold's car in the garage. Andy barely waited for the car to stop before jumping out and running toward the front door yelling, "Papa!"

Matt looked at Margaret and said, "He really loves that man, Margaret. I doubt if anything short of a miracle will separate them."

Margaret didn't answer out loud but thought to herself, *If a miracle is what it takes, then I will just have to come up with a miracle. Again* she wondered where that thought had come from but was quickly learning that her instincts were paying off. Her thoughts seemed to be keeping her focused on the steps she needed to take to control Andy's future.

Andrew and Andy walked toward the car. "Can I give you a hand unloading Andy's gear, Matt?" Andrew said.

"Thanks, but they are right here in the back. Andy did a great job of packing his things."

Andrew walked toward the passenger side of the car. Margaret rolled down the window and offered, "Hi, Dad. How was Portland?"

"Everything's hunky-dory, Maggie."

Margaret wanted to scowl at her father for using the familiar name Maggie but controlled herself and showed no sign of discontent.

"Come on in for a bit. I'll put on some coffee."

"Thanks anyway, Dad, but it's been a long day, and I have lots to do before tomorrow."

Matt walked over, gave Andy a shoulder hug, and said, "I had a great time, Andy. Hope we can do this again real soon."

"Me too, Uncle Matt. Maybe Papa can go next time."

Chapter Thirteen

Two months passed. Andy and Andrew had settled into a daily routine of Bible study in the mornings, followed by chores and some free time. One Wednesday night in late August, Andy went to his youth gathering at the church. Pastor Frank walked to the front of the room, and right behind him was John. Andy had a grin on his face as they caught each other's eye.

"I'd like to introduce our new youth pastor. This is Pastor John Staats. He graduated from Columbia Bible College and has been the assistant to Dr. Frum at the Cascade Academy in the Blue Mountains."

John walked up front as Pastor Frank took a seat. "First, I'd like you all to call me John. There isn't really that much of a difference in our age. It's important to me to guide you into a deeper walk in the spirit of our Lord and show you that walk can be both inspiring and fun. Are there any questions? I can't promise I'll have an answer, but I do promise to find one." When there was no response, John said, "Good. Let's eat." The mood immediately changed from solemn to excited as the young people attacked the cookies and juice.

John spotted Andy talking to a girl and went over to them. Andy said, "This is Laura, that's her twin brother Larry over by the food."

John extended his hand and said "Glad to meet you Laura. Have you been here long?"

"No! Actually, we just moved to Pasco a few months ago, and we really like it." Turning to Andy, John said, "It's really good to see you again, Andy. I was looking forward to it."

"Me too, John. But it's been such a busy summer that I kinda forgot about you coming here."

John laughed. "Guess you decided not to attend Cascade then, right?"

"You're right. Like I said, it wasn't my idea, but I'm glad we stopped. If we hadn't made that visit, I wouldn't have had the chance to meet you."

"I know what you mean. Seeing a familiar face makes me feel a lot more comfortable."

⬥ ⬥ ⬥ ⬥ ⬥ ⬥ ⬥ ⬥ ⬥ ⬥ ⬥ ⬥ ⬥ ⬥ ⬥ ⬥ ⬥ ⬥

Andrew was in the kitchen when Andy returned.

"Hey, Papa, guess what. John Staats was there tonight."

"And just who is John Staats?"

"He's the guy I told you about that I met at Cascade."

"What's Cascade? You've lost me."

Andy realized that he was so excited when he returned from his camping trip that he had forgotten to tell Andrew about the visit to the school. "You know what? I forgot to tell you about Aunt Margaret making an appointment for me to visit a school in the Blue Mountains she wanted me to check out."

Andrew grabbed a couple sodas, handed one to Andy, sat down, and said, "Tell me about it, Andy."

"Well, there is an academy in the Blue Mountains called Cascade. Margaret said it was a school where I could learn about things I won't learn at my high school. She said it would broaden my knowledge. Anyway, while we were there, the head guy—his name was Dr. Frum—had his assistant show me around. That was John Staats. He told me then that he had accepted the position of youth pastor at our church, but I had forgotten about it until tonight."

Andrew was quiet. It bothered him that Margaret had decided on her own to set up an appointment and hadn't bothered to mention it to him. He also had the feeling that since she hadn't mentioned it, there was probably a good reason.

"I think we should have this man over for pizza. What do you think?"

"Great idea, Papa. He said that since we had already met, my face was familiar, and it made it a lot easier to settle in a new place. He's staying in the old parsonage where Pastor Frank used to live. I'll stop by tomorrow and ask him."

· · · · · · · · · · · · · · · · · ·

John was digging up a neglected flower garden on the east side of the house when Andy drove up. "Hey, John, need some help?"

"Hi, Andy. Never turn down help. There's a rake leaning against the house."

Andy grabbed the rake and started smoothing out the overturned ground. "Want to come over tonight for pizza?"

"You bet. I was wondering who would take pity and offer to feed me." They worked in silence for a few minutes; then John said, "How did your aunt take it when you said you didn't want to go to Cascade?"

"Okay, I guess. She didn't say much about it and hasn't mentioned it since. I even forgot to tell my grandpa until last night."

It took about an hour to finish working the ground and planting the flowers John had purchased that morning. "Come on in and have some lemonade, Andy."

"Sounds good, but I think I'll take some water."

"Water it is."

They got their drinks and took them to the long, wide front porch with a porch swing, small wooden table, and three lawn chairs. Andy sat down on the swing, and John sat in a plastic lawn chair. John asked, "So did you inherit your papa's love for working the ground?"

Andy was stunned. The frown he gave John could have been mistaken as anger under different circumstances. "John, how did you know I called my grandfather 'Papa,' and how did you know he worked with the ground?"

John bent toward Andy and rested his arms on his legs. He stared into his lemonade for a few seconds before he answered. "I know a great deal about you, Andy, but there are many things that I can't explain to you right now. I can tell you that I'll be here for you any time you need me."

Andy wanted to probe deeper, but for some reason, the need to know more seemed to vanish. He finished his water and, after giving John directions to his house, said good-bye and left. It wasn't until he had gone inside and saw Andrew sitting in what had now become his favorite chair in the living room that he again wondered how John knew about his papa. He was about to say something to Andrew, but again, it didn't seem to be the thing to do.

"What did John say about pizza?"

"He said it was about time someone took pity on him and fed him," Andy answered with a grin. "I think he is going to be a great leader, Papa. He has a lot of insight."

"I sure hope so. I've been praying that God would send someone who was closer to your age to not only guide you in your future with God but someone you could do things with."

• • • • • • • • • • • • • • • • • • •

Life seemed to be returning to normal. There was an emptiness that Andy felt when something reminded him of his mom and dad, but even those times were becoming less and less frequent. He enjoyed time with John and found every excuse he could to spend time with Laura. They had gone to a couple of movies, but Larry and a date were always with them. They were sixteen but had a lot in common with Andy. Laura liked to camp, play baseball, and even fish.

It was Wednesday night and time to get ready for youth meeting. Andy looked forward to the fellowship he had with John and several new friends who had started attending youth night. Giving himself one more look in the mirror, he found his mind more on how Laura would appreciate the way he looked than his satisfaction.

The activity room was already full when he arrived. John was going over some music with Sandy, who played the piano for all the services at the church. Andy was looking around the room to see who was there, but he was really looking for Laura.

"Hi, Andy."

Andy turned around and again experienced a slight flush that was always present when he saw Laura. "Hi! Where's Larry?"

"He's parking the car. He let me out so I could find you and we could all sit together."

"Cool."

Larry, Laura, and Andy found seats in the front of the room just as John walked to the front.

"Hi, everyone. Wow! What a turnout. If this keeps up, we'll run out of room." There were a few muffled chuckles, as everyone knew the west wall was folding panels that opened into an equally large room. "Would anyone like to open with prayer?" When no one responded, John said, "Okay, you got me again. Let's all stand up and honor our Father."

When sounds of scraping chairs and a few coughs ended, John began. "Father, we are here to honor you in praise and worship. Our hearts are full of thanksgiving for your priceless gift of Jesus Christ, which offers not only salvation but also eternal life. Help us all to resolve to be obedient to your will, and lead us each minute of every day. Let your joy be part of this meeting tonight. In Jesus's name, amen.

"Okay, let's get started. Any praises to share?"

Laura quickly stood and said, "I am thankful that we found this church. We've made so many new friends and look forward to even closer friendships." Laura heard a few snickers; then it seemed like everyone in the room was roaring with laughter at Laura's final remark. Her attraction for Andy was no secret to anyone but Andy. Laura's face turned scarlet, and she wanted to run from the room, but she heard Andy say, "Me too, Laura." The two smiled at one another, and Laura sat down.

Andy stood up, and when everyone had quieted down, he said, "Laura is right. We all know how important Christian friendship can be and how dangerous it is when we lose touch. I, for one, don't know what I would do without all of you, these meetings, and John's guidance." The group sobered as each remembered times when they had been in situations they knew would not have happened if they had been with Christian friends.

⚬ ⚬ ⚬ ⚬ ⚬ ⚬ ⚬ ⚬ ⚬ ⚬ ⚬ ⚬ ⚬ ⚬ ⚬ ⚬ ⚬

When Andy got home, he knew Andrew would be waiting to ask how the meeting had gone, and he had already decided to ask if he could have a youth group party. Andrew was on the phone when Andy entered the kitchen and was surprised to hear Andrew say, "That sounds great, John. I'll talk it over with Andy and let you know."

After Andrew hung up the phone, he explained to Andy, "That was John. After the meeting one of the kids said she had asked her aunt about having a cookout for the group."

Andy should have been surprised, but since the phone call had been from John, he wasn't. "Which kid was it?"

"It wasn't Laura, was it?"

"As a matter of fact, I think it was. Sound like a good idea to you?"

"Sure, that was sort of what the meeting was all about tonight—Christian friends."

"Why don't you talk to John about it tomorrow? Maybe you can even offer to help Laura set it up."

● ● ● ● ● ● ● ● ● ● ● ● ● ● ● ● ● ● ●

Andy was waiting for John to answer the doorbell at ten o'clock the following morning. John yelled, "Come on in, Andy."

Andy grinned and, walking in, headed straight for the kitchen. John was sitting at the kitchen table with his open Bible.

"Studying anything particular, John?"

"I am doing a bit of research on Christian companionship."

"Follow up from last night's meeting, huh?"

"In a way. But I'm going a bit deeper than what we discussed last night."

"How come?"

"Because I don't think kids realize the real danger out there when it comes to who they associate with."

"Danger?"

"Yes, danger. God's Word has a lot to say about the dangers of a false or wrong friendship."

"Like what?"

"Well, take Job. He had three friends visit when he was afflicted, but what did he say? In Psalm 109:1–5 he asks God not to remain silent because deceitful men surround him. He goes on to say that they returned his friendship with accusations. You've heard the saying 'sunshine friend'? As long as Job was wealthy, healthy, and wise, they were right there to encourage and flatter. Now that Job's in trouble, they accuse him of wrongdoing. Job had many years of walking with God before his affliction, Andy—unlike most teenagers today. Now think about what would happen if a real good friend accused a marginal, teenage Christian of cheating, the authorities believed the friend, and the Christian was punished. He knows he wasn't guilty, but no one believed him. After all, they don't punish kids that haven't done something wrong. Ever heard 'I've served the time, might as well do the crime'?"

"Well, not exactly that way. Isn't it the other way around, John?"

"Not in this case. You see, at that age, the kid figures he's been labeled a cheat anyway. Job called them 'miserable comforters.' In a nice way, he told them to shut up and asked them what on earth was wrong with them. He said that if the table was turned and they were in trouble, he could say the miserable things to them that they were saying to him. Instead, he said he would comfort them (Job 16:2–5). Psalm 35:4–15 tells us about friends that we help out, only to have them turn on us when they think there is something to gain. Or how about when you trust a good friend, as David warns us in Psalm 55:12–14, that when an enemy comes against us, at least we know what to expect, right? How about someone who is a friend to your face and an enemy when your back is turned?"

"Whoa. I hope I never run into that kind of friend."

"I hope not too, but I can guarantee that you will."

Andy didn't say anything, but looking straight into John's eyes, he knew it was true. "Are there any more scriptures about friends, John?"

John laughed. "The surface has just been scratched, but here's some homework for you if you have some spare time: Proverbs 11:13 talks about gossip. Proverbs 17:9 talks about a friend who understands a mistake and doesn't condemn. Spend some time reading about how great a true friend is. Tell you what, how about giving a talk at a youth group on Proverbs 27:6, about how you can trust a friend that tells you the truth even if it hurts but an enemy will just go along with you on something that is wrong."

"Okay. Guess you've noticed I don't have a problem being the center of attention," Andy answered with a grin.

"Since this is so important, there are things you and your friends need to think about Andy."

"Can you give me some examples?"

"The difference between real love and infatuation. Having a friend that would put themselves in harm's way for you.""Do you have a friend like that?"

"Yeah, I know Papa would."

"One that's really hard to deal with is when we are young, we want to please others and be on the inside. It's very difficult to be excluded. Ha! That's hard no matter what age you are."

"That kind of happened to me. After one of our baseball games, the team went down to the river and started drinking. I joined them once and really had fun, but the look on Dad's face when I got home was one I'll never forget. He didn't say anything to me, but he didn't have to. I never went back to the river, and the team gave me a bunch of crap for it. There were other things the team did, but they wouldn't ask me.

"Hey, the reason I came over here was to talk to you about a cookout. Sounds like it fits right in with what we were just talking about."

"In a way, Andy, yes. I suggested that we have our next youth meeting at the cookout. Everyone I've talked to agrees."

"It sounds like a great idea." Andy continued, "Hey, I better get going. Didn't mean to waste your whole morning."

"Hold on, Andy. One thing you have to know about me is that talking with someone about the Word is never a waste of my time. It's priority one, and no matter what time of day or night, if you have a question, I'll be there with an answer; I promise."

Andy thought John had come on a bit strong but felt a comfort in what he said. "At this point, John, I consider you a friend and trust you." Andy felt a bit awkward but extended his hand to John as if to shake in a pact of friendship. John took Andy's hand, but instead of shaking hands, John held Andy's hand and quoted the benediction. "The LORD bless you and keep you; the LORD make his face shine upon you and be gracious to you; the LORD turn his face toward you and give you peace." Numbers 6:24–26.

Andy's hand, arm, and shoulder were tingling as if he had touched a low-voltage wire. He wanted to jerk his hand free but couldn't.

When John finally turned loose of Andy's hand, he was grinning from ear to ear. "The Holy Spirit can give us a real jolt when he wants to be noticed."

"How did you know? How do you know it was the Holy Spirit?"

"I just do."

"Gotta go. See you next Saturday at the cookout. I'm not sure where it's going to be. I guess Laura is in charge of finding a place, and I'll let you know as soon as I talk to her."

Andy thought about all that John had said as he drove home. The importance of friendships was something he hadn't really thought much about. He knew it was a subject he had to study.

⦾　⦾　⦾　⦾　⦾　⦾　⦾　⦾　⦾　⦾　⦾　⦾　⦾　⦾　⦾　⦾

Andy entered his house with his usual shout: "Hey, Papa. I'm home."

"Hi, Andy. Did you talk to John about the cookout?"

"Yeah, sure did. We got into a discussion about what the Bible says about friendships."

"The Word has many warnings about friends, Andy."

"I know that now. Before this morning, I didn't realize how much the Bible said about friends. I've got a lot of studying to do. John wants me to give a talk on the subject at one of our youth group meetings."

The phone interrupted their conversation. Andy was surprised to hear Laura's voice on the other end.

"Hi, Andy. I think I've found the perfect place for our cookout."

"Oh yeah? Where?"

"The lady my aunt cleans for told me we could have it in her backyard. It's a really neat place with a pool and everything."

"That's great, Laura. Where is it?"

"It belongs to Mr. And Mrs. Selby."

Andy was surprised and quiet long enough for Laura to say, "Hey, Andy, are you still there? Hello?"

"Yes, Laura, I'm still here. Guess the subject of who your aunt cleaned for never came up."

"Why should that make a difference?"

"If that is Matt and Margaret Selby, they are my aunt and uncle."

"Cool! You should feel right at home then."

Andy had an uneasy feeling but answered, "Yeah, I will. Do you want me to start calling the other kids to let them know?"

"That would be great. Larry said he would help. It should be a lot of fun."

Andy didn't know why, but he felt uneasy about having a youth group get-together at Margaret's. Why would she give her permission? Unless she hadn't been told it was a group of Christian kids…

He hung up the phone and went to find Andrew. Andrew was sitting in the blue recliner that had become "his" chair. He looked at Andy and knew something was wrong.

"Who was that on the phone?"

"It was Laura. She called to tell me that she had found a place to have the cookout."

"Great."

"I'm not so sure. Laura said her aunt cleans houses and one of her clients gave her permission to have the cookout in her backyard."

"That doesn't sound so bad."

"Well, it really isn't, except the people Laura's aunt works for is Aunt Margaret."

Andrew's instinct told him there was something going on that went a lot deeper than Margaret's kind-hearted offer.

"Andy, did you ask Laura how the subject came up about the cookout with Margaret?"

Andy shook his head and answered, "No. I didn't think about it at the time. Papa, would you call Aunt Margaret for me?"

"For what reason?"

"Well," Andy started slowly, "I guess Aunt Margaret should think you're calling to thank her for letting us use her backyard, but I think she should know that these kids are all Christians. Knowing how Aunt Margaret feels about church and stuff, it's hard for me to believe that she offered to let us meet there if she knew who all would be coming."

Andrew had thought about the same question and answered Andy with, "I think it's a good idea. But since it's your youth group, it would be better coming from you."

Andy was afraid this would be Andrew's position and quietly answered, "You're right, as usual."

Andy waited until seven thirty to call, hoping his aunt and uncle would both be home. He didn't want to do this more than once. Margaret answered on the second ring in her usual lawyer tone. "Margaret Selby."

"Aunt Margaret, this is Andy."

"Well, hello, Andy! It's been awhile since we've heard your voice. Is everything okay?"

"Everything's fine over here. I just heard the news today from Laura that her aunt cleans house for you and you gave her permission to let Laura have a cookout in your backyard."

"Well, yes, Andy. It sounds like it should be a lot of fun."

"Oh, I'm sure it will. I just want you to know that the church's youth group really appreciates your offer and we all thank you a lot."

The other end of the line was silent just a split second too long; then she said, "Andy, did you think that we didn't know the cookout was for your church youth group?"

"Well, err…I didn't know for sure."

Margaret gave a slight chuckle and answered, "It's fine, Andy. Yes, we did know who would be coming, including you." Margaret hesitated, and Andy remained silent. "You need to know something, Andy. Uncle Matt and I may not agree with some of your beliefs, but we want to support you any way we can. There is nothing particularly harmful and certainly not immoral about your lifestyle, and if you choose to make Christianity the focus of your life, then we need to respect that."

*Andy heard what his aunt was saying, but something deep inside caused doubt and even worse, fear. Andy finally answered Margaret, "Aunt Margaret, thanks again. I'm glad you knew who would be coming before you gave your permission. It makes me feel good that you would do this for the group."

"More specifically, Andy, we did it for *your* group."

"Well, there will be about five of us coming over next Saturday to set up for the party and do a little decorating. Don't worry, we'll make sure everything is spic and span before we leave after the party."

Margaret laughed. "Don't worry about it. I'm sure you'll all have a great time. We're having the pool cleaned early Friday morning, and we dug some old Japanese lanterns out of the attic for you to use if you want them."

"That's great. Good-bye!"

Andy hung up the phone and wondered if Margaret's offer was really on the up-and-up. He sat on the sofa across from Andrew, and the two men silently looked at each other with the same question shouting into the silence.

"So what do you think, Andy? I heard your end of the conversation."

"I'm not sure what to think, Papa. Guess we'll just have to wait until Saturday and see."

Chapter Fourteen

Saturday was a beautiful, warm day. Larry, Laura, and Ben were attaching ropes to trees and poles for the lanterns Margaret had left on the patio table. When Andy turned the corner of the house, Laura shouted hello and started to walk toward him. She heard her brother yell, "Oh no, you don't! Get back here and hold this ladder for me." Laura grinned at Andy, shrugged, and said, "Duty calls," as she returned to the bottom of the ladder.

"Wow! The yard looks great, you guys. What time did you start, anyway?"

"We were here at six thirty. Didn't you get the message I left on your answering machine?" Ben yelled back.

"No. Sorry, guys. Grandpa and I went downtown and grabbed a pizza last night, and I didn't check the machine before I went to bed."

"That's okay, Andy," Laura said. "There really wasn't that much to do. Your aunt had everything pretty well done already."

"'Your aunt?'" asked Larry as he started down the ladder.

"Yes. I didn't know either until Andy told me, but Mr. And Mrs. Selby are Andy's aunt and uncle," answered Laura.

"Bet you spend a lot of time in that great pool, huh, Andy?"

"Not really. I really haven't had much time."

"What do you mean? How long have they lived here?"

Andy didn't want to get into family history with his friends but wasn't sure how to avoid explaining the association.

"How about some refreshments?" came from the kitchen door leading onto the patio.

"Speaking of aunts…hi, Aunt Mable!" Larry shouted back.

"You bet. Always ready for food," Ben said as he headed toward the table.

Andy couldn't take his eyes off of Laura. Every time she looked at him, he felt like he had been caught doing something wrong. Laura just smiled and turned her attention to someone else. When the yard was finished, Ben, Larry, Laura, and Andy stood back and admired their work, said they would see each other at six, and left the Selbys.'

Andy's mind was muddled. He decided to stop by John's house on his way home. John was sitting on the porch with his coffee and his Bible. As Andy walked toward the porch, he wondered why he needed to see John and what he would say.

"Hi, Andy. I've been waiting for you."

Andy's foot was on the first step, but John's greeting stopped him cold. "What do you mean you've been waiting for me?"

John just smiled and said, "Come on up and sit down. Would you like something to drink?"

"No thanks. I just had something at Aunt Margaret's. We just finished decorating the yard for the party tonight. It really looks good."

John didn't say anything more; he waited for Andy to tell him the real reason for his visit. Andy knew John well enough now to know he was waiting for him to ask the question. The problem was, Andy didn't know the question. Both men sat quietly waiting for the other to say something.

"How does God feel about women?" Andy was shocked at his outburst and the stupidity of his question. John wanted to answer Andy's question, but when he tried, all he could do was laugh. Andy soon joined in, and both men laughed so hard that tears were rolling down their faces.

When John finally gained control, he said, "I think you mean, 'How does God feel about relationships between a man and a woman?'"

"Yeah," Andy answered, a little embarrassed.

John became very serious. He finally said, "God created men and women for that very reason." John waited a few seconds for his answer to register with Andy then continued, "Relationships between people take many forms, but the relationship between a man and a woman is very special to God. Men and women can form a unique friendship bond, supporting and encouraging one another. There is the beautiful relationship between husband and wife. I've heard about the eulogy you gave at your folks' funeral, so I know you've witnessed that relationship firsthand."

Andy said nothing but shook his head in agreement as he had visions of the times when he saw his mom and dad share spontaneous acts of caring and tenderness.

John continued, "There are two forces at work in everything that touches our lives: good and evil, constructive and destructive, love and hate. So how are we to know when a relationship is one that God ordained or just allowed?"

"Yeah, that's the question I meant to ask," Andy said with relief and a deep gratitude that he had a friend that knew just what to say.

John grinned. "Tell me about your past experiences with women, Andy."

The question surprised Andy, and he was embarrassed but answered, "I've had girlfriends, but they were just for fun. We went to school dances, did youth group things together in the church, and went to a few movies…you know, that sort of thing. I've held a girl's hand and…" Andy hesitated but finally blurted out, "…even kissed a girl a couple of times."

"Those were crushes. But I think we're talking about something a little more than a crush between you and Laura, aren't we?"

Andy's mouth dropped open. "How do you know these things? How did you know I was talking about Laura?"

John leaned toward Andy. "Because it's obvious. There was a spark between you two the first time you laid eyes on one another." John waited a minute then said, "Remember one thing, Andy—if it doesn't seem or feel right, it probably isn't."

Andy didn't understand this at all. He knew that there had been things in his life that didn't feel right but turned out to be God's will. "I don't understand."

"We can't be held accountable for decisions that are out of our control. A parent that tells a child to do something that seems wrong, a friend that makes the choice to do something you know is wrong, or God's decision to allow something that we think was wrong are all things that seem wrong but we can't control."

"That makes sense. But what has that got to do with me and Laura?"

John simply answered, "The decisions you make with Laura are in your control."

Andy knew what John meant. He thought about the fantasies he had about he and Laura. He thought about the exhilarating feeling he had when he thought about being with Laura, the excitement he felt when he knew he would see her. Andy lowered and shook his head.

John said, "Andy, do you remember the scriptures I gave you to read about infatuation and real love? I think the story about Samson and Delilah is a good picture of infatuation and lust. On the other hand, the Song of Solomon is a beautiful story of true love. Most people fall somewhere in between.

"Let's look at some questions to see if we can find an example in this story that may tie into your questions. Why didn't he tell her the truth in the beginning? After Samson was set upon the third time, don't you think he may have had a clue that something was wrong? Why do you think God allowed all this to happen?" John decided to wait for Andy to answer some or all of these questions.

Andy answered, "You know, Samson did some dumb stuff, but I don't think he was dumb. He disobeyed God by associating with Delilah and ignored all the warning signs. Even though he knew it was wrong, he didn't care. One great thing about Laura is that she is a Christian and that's important to me. I don't think I need to worry about her and I haven't had any warning signs yet"

"That's right, Andy. God's Word tells us in Proverbs 12:15 that the way of a fool seems right to him, but a wise man listens to advice. If you are walking with our Lord and Savior, seeking his will in all your ways, leaning on his knowledge in all situations and not your understanding, you'll hear his advice when you need it. As I said before, if it doesn't seem right, it probably isn't."

Andy admired John's wisdom and told him so. He stood up and extended his hand toward John. John also stood and, recognizing the meaning behind the gesture, enfolded Andy's hand with both of his hands, each man realizing the importance of the bond between them.

It was after three when Andy finally pulled into his driveway. Andrew was weeding a flower bed along the front walk. Andy called out, "Who's winning, Papa?"

Andrew laughed. "I am. It feels good to get my hands in the dirt."

"Do you miss farming that much, Papa?"

"No. Farming is a little different. You worry about nature's balance, crop failure or abundance, equipment breaking down or lasting one more season, and whether you will make money or lose money for a year of hard work. Man's first duty was to tend God's garden, and isn't it interesting that when we work in the earth with our hands, we are usually on our knees?"

Andy laughed. "Never thought about it that way."

"Are you all ready for the party tonight?"

"Yeah. We finished about noon, but I stopped by John's on the way home."

Andrew just smiled and said, "That's good." Then he turned his attention back to weeding.

Andy walked toward the house, asking himself if he would ever have the amazing insight of John and his papa. They not only seemed to know the answers but knew the question before he even had a chance to ask. Andrew always seemed to know what was happening in Andy's life either before it happened or while it was happening and whether it was a good thing or a bad thing.

Chapter Fifteen

Most of the kids were already at the party and eating when Andy walked around the corner of the Selby house. Laura saw Andy and ran over to him. "Doesn't the yard look fantastic, Andy?" Laura said.

"It looks like something out of a fairy tale, and so do you." Andy thought Laura was beautiful in her ankle-length full skirt that looked like something a Spanish dancer would wear.

Laura blushed. "It's because of you, Andy. You bring out the best in me."

Before Andy could say any more, Larry yelled, "Hey, you two better get over here and grab a plate while there's some food left."

On the way to the table, Laura grabbed Andy's hand and, lowering her voice, said, "Hey, Andy, after we eat, I need to talk to you in private. I have a favor to ask."

The table looked like the party was almost over instead of just starting. Andy chuckled and said to Larry, "I see what you mean about the food." Just as Andy finished his comment to Larry, a cart rolled out of the kitchen door full of hamburger patties, chips, baked beans, hot corn on the cob, cakes, cookies, pop, and punch. "Wow!" was all Andy and Larry could say. He laughed and added, "Never thought I'd see the day when *ants* rescued a picnic, but our *aunts* sure have—pun intended."

Both boys filled their plates and sat down next to Laura at one of the picnic tables. They were joined by several other kids who were on their second, some on their third, plates of food, and they talked about returning to school.

When they finished eating, Andy stood up, looked at Laura, and, extending his hand for her to take, said, "Excuse us, guys." Everyone grinned as they watched Laura and Andy walk toward a gazebo that stood at the end of a concrete walk lined on both sides by blue and white pansies. Unknown to all was the unseen person watching the two through binoculars from a second-floor window of the house. It was still light enough to make out who it was, and the lanterns made it easy to see what they were doing.

Margaret watched as Andy and Laura stood face-to-face, holding hands. She had one hand holding the binoculars and one hand on a pager button. She saw Laura say something to Andy and saw Andy shake his head like he was agreeing with her. Laura started to reach inside her skirt pocket, and Margaret pushed the pager button.

Before Laura pulled a package from her pocket, Andy had wrapped his arms around her and kissed her.

Laura gasped, forgot about the package she had for Andy, and returned his kiss.

Andy heard John's voice asking if anyone had seen him. He also heard a couple of his friends yell back, "Try the gazebo!" Andy stepped back and said, "Wait a minute. I'll be right back."

"Hey, John! I was wondering if you were going to make it." Andy was walking toward John, and they met about halfway between the gazebo and the pool.

John smiled at Andy. "I see you're exploring relationships."

Andy grinned. "Kind of."

Before anything more was said, they heard someone shout, "We're looking for Andy Staple! Anyone seen him?"

Kids started pointing toward Andy and John and opening a pathway for the men. Margaret came running out of the house, demanding to know what was going on. There were four men—three in policemen's uniforms and one in a blue suit. Two policemen stood back and watched the kids in the yard, and one officer stood beside the fourth man. As the man in the blue suit pulled a thin wallet from his coat pocket, a fear that bordered on panic hit Andy as he remembered the last time he had seen a man in a dark suit pull a thin wallet from his pocket. The first thing that ran through Andy's mind was that something had happened to his papa. He ran toward the men, shouting, "I'm Andy Staple! What's wrong?"

The two men looked surprised, and their official demeanor softened. The man in the blue suit said, "We have a couple of questions to ask you, Andy." Addressing Margaret, he continued, "Is there somewhere we can talk in private?"

Margaret nodded her head toward the house, but as John approached, he heard her say, "Before this goes any further, I want you to know that I'm an attorney, and with his permission, I will offer Andy legal counsel." Margaret looked at Andy for confirmation and permission.

Andy was still stunned but answered, "Sure, Aunt Margaret. If you think I need it."

Margaret stuttered as she answered, "It's just in case, Andy." At that moment, Margaret glanced up to see John staring at her, and their eyes locked. She turned toward the house and said, "Follow me." As the last person in the foursome entered the house, Margaret glanced back and saw that John had not taken his eyes off of her. She led the group into Matt's den and closed the door. "Now, what's this all about?"

The man in the blue suit said to Andy, "I'm Detective Dan Paulsen, son, and this is Officer Akers."

Andy could stand it no longer. He blurted out, "Is my papa okay?"

The two men were surprised and answered, "No one is hurt, Andy. This is about something else."

Andy let out a loud sigh of relief and slumped into his Uncle Matt's brown leather chair.

Detective Paulsen continued, "Andy, do you know Dean Thompson?"

Andy thought a minute then answered slowly, "That name sounds familiar. There are some new kids in our church youth group that didn't come to the party."

"This is a party for a bunch of church kids?"

"Yeah, our 'summer's almost over' party. Why?"

"Well, err…we just didn't expect that one."

Margaret had stayed silent long enough. "Just what is going on, gentlemen?"

"Dean Thompson has implicated Andy in a cocaine transaction, Mrs. Selby."

Margaret's reaction was one of immediate outrage. "Just what backs up this term of 'implicated,' Mr. Paulsen?"

"Dean told us that he made arrangements to sell Andy a small package of cocaine and we would find the proof here tonight."

"And do you have a search warrant?"

Officer Akers answered, "Do we need one, counselor?" This caught Margaret off guard.

Before anything more was said, Detective Paulsen said, "As a matter of fact, we do, Mrs. Selby." Margaret appeared to be deep in thought as Detective Paulsen said, "We would like to search you, Andy."

Margaret started to protest, but Andy answered the detective while standing with his arms outstretched as if he waited for crucifixion. Paulsen nodded to Officer Akers, and Akers started searching Andy.

Akers finally stood up and announced that Andy was clean. Paulsen and Margaret exchanged quick glances.

Margaret said, "Is there anything else?"

"I'm afraid we're going to have to search the premises. Have any of the kids been in the house?"

"No. One of the rules for using the yard was that no one was to enter the house except the maid or myself. My husband is out of town on business."

"What about the bathroom?"

"There is a restroom in the pool house. I'll say it again—none of the kids have been in the house."

Paulsen gave a nodding signal to Akers to begin a search of the property. Akers left the room, and Paulsen turned to Andy. "Andy, is there any reason you can think of why anyone would want to get you in trouble?"

"No, sir…unless…" Andy continued after a brief pause, "What did you say the guy's name was again?"

"Dean Thompson. Mean anything to you?"

"I think so. There was a Dean that played on our baseball team at school. The team was pretty mad at me when I decided not to play this year. I don't want to sound like I'm boasting, Detective, but the coach said that if I didn't play this year, the team probably wouldn't make it to state. I went through some pretty rough days at school after my folks died and having the baseball team mad at me."

"Wait a minute. Your last name is Staple, right? Were your folks Harold and Sarah?"

"Yes. Did you know them?"

"Your dad better than your mom, but I know they were good Christian, law-abiding people."

Paulsen stared at Margaret so hard her cheeks turned red. Margaret's reaction wasn't because the detective knew Harold; most people in the Pasco business world did know him. She was more distressed because the detective had mentioned that he knew Harold was a Christian.

Someone knocked on the door. "Yes! Come in!" Margaret shouted.

Two policemen entered the room with Laura between them. One of the policemen handed Paulsen a small package wrapped in gift paper suitable for a wedding. Laura said nothing and stared at the floor.

"Found this package on this young lady, sir."

Paulsen took the package and asked Laura, "Want to tell me what's in the package?"

"I don't really know. A kid from school asked me to give it to Andy tonight."

"Wait a minute, Laura. You said Uncle Matt bought a present for my aunt and wanted you to give it to me to hold until their anniversary next week."

Laura didn't look up or answer Andy's question.

"Well, young lady, which is it?"

"It's like I said, a kid at school said he wanted to play a joke on Andy, you know, like a senior prank…" Laura began to stumble over her words as she continued, "He told me it was wrapped like a present so I could make up a story about where it came from. They didn't want Andy to figure out who really sent it."

Laura finally looked up at Andy. Her face was wet with tears, and through her sobs she cried, "I'm so sorry, Andy. I thought it was a joke and everyone would have a big laugh. I had no idea there was dope involved."

Paulsen looked at Akers then at Margaret. He said to Laura, "You just made a big mistake, miss."

"What do you mean?"

"No one said anything about dope. Mrs. Selby, Officer Akers, and Andy were the only ones in this room when I said why we were here."

The room was charged with Andy's hurt, Margaret's disgust, and Laura's fear. Paulsen said, "Call CPA. As soon as they get here, take her downtown. Make sure you contact her folks, and hold her for more questions. I can't see any reason to detain Andy right now." He looked at Andy and finished with, "Stay available, Andy. We will have more questions."

Margaret said, "Laura and her twin brother, Larry, live with their aunt, who happens to be my housekeeper. She's just outside. I'll let her know what's going on, and I will be representing Laura. Right, Laura?"

Laura looked up and, in barely more than a whisper, said, "Right."

"For right now, Laura, you are not to say anything. Understand? Nothing. I'll come down to headquarters as soon as I close down the party and make some arrangements. Okay?"

"Okay, Mrs. Selby."

Andy found himself standing alone in his uncle's den. He was almost numb and more than a little confused about what had just happened. He looked up and saw John standing at the door. "You okay, Andy?"

"I think so." Andy told John everything that had been said in the den and added, "What just happened here?"

John hesitated before he answered Andy then said, "It appears that someone tried to separate you from the source of your strength."

● ● ● ● ● ● ● ● ● ● ● ● ● ● ● ● ●

When Andy got home, he was surprised to see his grandfather on his knees in the living room. Running over to Andrew, Andy fell down beside him and said, "What's wrong, Papa?"

Andrew looked at Andy with red-rimmed eyes then threw his arms around his grandson and wept. When Andrew calmed down, he held Andy at arm's length and said, "It appears that our God has come through for us one more time, Andy." Andy helped his papa up from the floor to his chair. Andrew asked Andy to sit down and explain what had happened at Margaret's house.

"You know, Papa, I'm not really sure what happened. We were eating, laughing, and having a good time when Laura said she had something for me, and we went to the gazebo." Andy stopped to think through the events for a second then continued, "The next thing I knew, some policemen were looking for me. We went into Uncle Matt's den, and they wanted to search me. I told them that there was no problem or reason why they shouldn't. They all looked surprised when they didn't find anything. The really confusing thing was that they brought Laura in and said they found a package in her pocket. Laura said a kid at school asked her to give it to me as a joke, but she messed up by saying she didn't know it was dope. No one had said anything about it being narcotics, so she had to know what it was." Tears ran down Andy's face, and he leaned back, closed his eyes, and sobbed.

Andrew went to the couch and wrapped Andy in his arms. He told Andy that he was at his friend's house for just a few minutes when there was a real urgency for him to come home and pray. "How did you know what to pray for, Papa?"

Andrew cupped Andy's face with his two hands and answered, "I had no need to know, Andy. God knew what was happening, and the Spirit prayed for you through me."

The doorbell rang. Andrew said, "I'll get it, Andy. I was expecting this visit." Andrew's statement puzzled Andy, but he stayed on the couch while Andrew went to the door. Before the door was completely open, Andrew said, "Come in, Margaret."

As Margaret stepped inside, she said, "Did Andy tell you what happened at the party, Dad?"

"He's told me a little, but maybe you can fill me in."

Margaret wasn't sure where to start, so she asked, "What has Andy told you so far?"

Andrew knew Margaret was on a fishing expedition, so he answered, "He said something about the police at your house looking for drugs and his friend Laura being arrested."

Margaret answered, "That's about all I know too right now. I'm on my way to the police department now to talk to Laura but wanted to stop by and make sure Andy was okay."

Andrew offered, "Maybe I should come down with you to see if I can get some answers."

"I think you should stay here with Andy. He was pretty shaken up when he left the house."

"You're right; you can let me know what you find out."

Margaret gave a quick glance into the living room and saw Andy lying on the couch with his arm over his eyes. She gave her dad a quick squeeze on the arm and left.

Andrew closed the door and quietly walked back into the living room shaking his head. He sat down in his chair, and neither of them had anything to say.

Finally Andy said, "I think Aunt Margaret knew something was going to happen, Papa."

Andrew wasn't sure how he should respond to Andy's statement. He remained silent.

The doorbell rang again. This time Andy sat up and said, "I've been expecting this one, Papa." He walked to the door.

John stood at the door with a look of pain that only comes from deep sorrow. Andy didn't say anything as he stepped back, indicating that John should enter and follow him back to the living room.

"Hello, John. It's good to see you again. I just wish the circumstances weren't so bad."

"Hello, Andrew. I think there is a need for some very serious prayer where there are two or more. There are no other two people that I know in this town that can get the job done as well as you two."

"What's happened, John?"

"I went to the police station to see if I could help Larry, Laura, and their aunt. They had Laura in a side room waiting for Margaret to get there. Larry and I were sitting out in the main entrance area. We heard the dispatcher ask a couple of detectives to go help the policemen at the Fourth Street overpass. It seems a car that had taken the Fourth Street ramp off the freeway went over the embankment. My sadness for the driver turned to fear when I heard the name of the driver was Dean Thompson."

Andy sat up with a bolt when he heard the name.

Andrew said, "That name mean something to you, Andy?"

"Yeah, it does, Papa. That's the name of the kid Laura said gave her the package that she was supposed to give me at the party tonight."

"You're right, John. There needs to be some very serious prayer for everyone involved with this."

John knelt down in front of the couch and buried his face in his hands. Andy knelt down beside him while Andrew knelt in front of his chair. A strange peace filled the room as each man quietly reflected on what had brought them together this night. John began praying aloud with, "Lord, we stand firm on your unchangeable Word. You've told us that if two on earth agree about anything, it will be done for us by your Father in heaven. We stand firm on that promise, Lord, as we seek your guidance and protection."

Andy expected John to continue in his prayer as he had done so many times at youth church but quickly became aware that instead of prayer, John was quoting Scripture. He continued with:

Hear me, O God, as I voice my complaint; protect my life from the threat of the enemy. Hide me from the conspiracy of the wicked, from that noisy crowd of evildoers. They sharpen their tongues like swords and aim their words like deadly arrows.

They shoot from ambush at the innocent man; they shoot at him suddenly, without fear.

They encourage each other in evil plans, they talk about hiding their snares; they say, "Who will see them?" They plot injustice and say, "We have devised a perfect plan!" Surely the mind and heart of man are cunning. But God will shoot them with arrows; suddenly they will be struck down. He will turn their own tongues against them and bring them to ruin; all who see them will shake their heads in scorn.

Psalm 64:1–8

John continued with:

But let all who take refuge in you be glad; let them ever sing for joy. Spread your protection over them that those who love your name may rejoice in you. For surely, O Lord, you bless the righteous; you surround them with your favor as with a shield.

Psalm 5:11–12

When John stopped, Andy felt a little guilty as he realized he was staring at John as he prayed. The feeling was short-lived when he heard the sobs of his grandfather. Andy knew why Andrew sobbed. He knew the enemy was none other than his papa's own Maggie. He knew in his heart that Andrew was in full agreement with John's petition, but he also knew it was breaking Andrew's heart. All Andy could say was, "I don't know what to say, Lord. I don't know how to help."

The room was silent. Andy was aware of movement in the room. He opened his eyes but saw nothing. Closing his eyes again, he waited for John or Andrew to continue praying. No one spoke. There it was again. This time it sounded like the noise of a gentle breeze blowing through treetops. Andy again opened his eyes and for a split second thought they had prayed all night, as the room was as bright as a summer's day. John and Andrew also opened their eyes to a familiar sight.

A voice of reassuring gentleness filled the room. John and Andrew bowed their heads in anticipation while Andy's eyes searched the room for the light source. They all heard the message that began, "My promises stand true for all my children. I am He that promises; I am He that is true; I am He that is no respecter of persons, therefore:

> "Because he loves me," says the LORD, "I will rescue him; I will protect him, for he acknowledges my name. He will call upon me, and I will answer him; I will be with him in trouble, I will deliver him and honor him. With long life will I satisfy him and show him my salvation."
>
> Psalm 91:14–16

The message continued,

> For the LORD gives wisdom, and from his mouth come knowledge and understanding. He holds victory in store for the upright; he is a shield to those whose walk is blameless, for he guards the course of the just and protects the way of his faithful ones. Then you will understand what is right and just and fair—every good path. For wisdom will enter your heart, and knowledge will be pleasant to your soul. Discretion will protect you, and understanding will guard you. Wisdom will save you from the ways of wicked men, from men whose words are perverse, who leave the straight paths to walk in dark ways, who delight in doing wrong and rejoice in the perverseness of evil, whose paths are crooked and who are devious in their ways.
>
> Proverbs 2:6–15

Andy was very quiet, waiting for more, but all he heard were his papa's sobs and quiet prayer, "Lord God, save my little Maggie."

John was the first to stand, followed by Andrew. He was aware of a hand on his shoulder and saw John standing over him, one hand lifted toward heaven, and with eyes still closed, he simply finished with, "Thank you, Father."

Andrew sat down in his chair, John sat on the couch, and Andy stood up but had no idea what to do. John and Andrew exchanged the very slightest smile, knowing the dilemma Andy felt. Andrew said, "I'm going to put on some tea," and walked into the kitchen.

John said, "Go ahead and ask me, Andy."

Used to John's ability to read his mind, Andy said, "What just happened here? I've never heard anyone quote Scripture instead of praying. That was really awesome. Is that how we should pray all the time?"

"No. Jesus taught us to acknowledge the Father, praise him, and ask for his forgiveness and for our daily needs. But these topics take many forms. Some just use the Lord's Prayer, some are just general, and some are very specific about their needs. But you should always be aware that God's words are always true. They were true for those we see in the Old Testament who loved God, and they are just as true for those who love God today. There are some tests the righteous of heart may ask of God—Gideon with his fleece, for example."

"Yes, but didn't Jesus say, 'Do not put the Lord your God to the test'?"

"Yes, he did. But do you remember who Jesus was speaking to at the time?"

"Oh, yeah. Satan, right?"

"That's right. And Satan did and does not have a heart for the Father. If you ask for a sign from the Father to make sure you are in his will in your requests and actions, why would you not expect him to give you an answer?"

"Got one more question. I don't know how, but I know you and Papa heard the same thing I did. How come you and Papa were so calm? It's not like you hear a voice come out of nowhere every day, and it's still a mystery how you can hear something so loud but there is no actual sound."

"I know you have heard the still, small voice of God, Andy, so you know what it means to hear with your spirit."

Andy stared into space, remembering the morning he had heard from his heavenly Father. He shook his head, affirming John's statement.

"God could have spoken to each of our hearts, but then we would have had to compare notes, right? God is practical; if there are several in the room, they all are asking the same question, and the answer is the same for everyone, why wouldn't he speak so that everyone could hear? By the way, do you know how to test a message from God?"

"Not really. Just believe it?"

"Never. The only way you can put a message to the test of truth is if what was said is in agreement with God's Word down to the last syllable."

"Was it?" Andy asked.

John took a pad and pencil from his coat pocket, wrote something down, and, handing it to Andy, said, "Before you go to sleep tonight, I want you to look up these two scriptures."

Andy read Psalm 91:14–16 and Proverbs 2:6–15.

Andrew yelled, "Come on into the kitchen and have some tea." Andrew had three cups of tea poured, and they all sat down. Andrew looked at John and said, "What do we do now?"

"We obey and wait on the Lord."

The phone rang. Andrew answered, "Hello!"

"Hi, Dad. This is Margaret."

"Margaret, what's happening?" Margaret was quiet. Andrew knew something was wrong. "What's wrong, Margaret?"

"I'm being held for questioning."

"Why?" Andrew knew the answer but wanted to give Margaret the chance to say what was on her mind.

"Laura told the police that Dean told her the whole thing was my idea and I had given him a lot of money to give Laura the package."

"Is that true?"

"Of course not, Dad. You know I would never do anything to hurt Andy. Anyway, they gave me one phone call. I wasn't sure I could get a hold of anyone in my law firm at this hour. Will you call my office first thing in the morning and get Dave down here by ten? They have to release me by then, and there are some papers I want Dave to file."

"Yes. I'll call first thing in the morning."

Margaret thanked Andrew, and they hung up. Andrew suddenly felt very old and very tired. He turned to John and Andy, who were watching him and waiting to hear the news.

"It seems that Laura implicated Margaret in this scheme, and she is being held for questioning."

Neither man looked surprised. They were all amazed at the speedy work of God. Andy's concern was for Andrew. "What do you want to do, Papa?"

"I don't know. Guess we'll just do as John said and wait on the Lord and see what his next step is."

John stood up. "We've done what I was sent here to do, so I'm going home to get some sleep. I'll see both of you tomorrow."

Chapter Sixteen

Andrew dozed off and on for the remainder of the night. By eight o'clock the next morning, he was showered and dressed. He called Margaret's office and asked to speak to Dave. After a short pause he heard, "Hello, Mr. Staple. How can I help you?"

"Hello, Dave. Margaret called last night and said she was being held at the police station. She said that even though they couldn't hold her for very long, there were some documents she wanted you to file. Anyway, she asked if you could be there by ten this morning."

Dave was quiet with shock. "What happened?"

Andrew didn't really want to go through it again and answered, "There was a mix-up involving some narcotics at a party at Margaret's house last night."

"Good God, Andrew! Thank you for calling. I'll get right down there and talk to Margaret." Andrew winched at the use of God's name being used in that manner but knew it was indicative of the environment surrounding Margaret's life.

Andrew made two more calls that morning and finished as Andy stumbled into the kitchen, rubbing his eyes. "Morning, Papa!"

"Good morning, Andy. Did you sleep last night?"

"A little. I feel like I just finished the first day of football practice."

"Know what you mean. I have a couple of errands to run. Will you be all right for a couple of hours?"

"Sure. Are you going down to see Aunt Margaret?"

"No, not right now. Her lawyer friends are on their way down there."

Saying nothing more, Andrew picked up the keys and walked out the front door.

· · · · · · · · · · · · · · · · · · · ·

Andrew pulled up in front of John's house and found John sitting on the front porch. John and Andrew had a cup of coffee and talked about what had happened the night before for a few minutes.

"There's something very important I'd like to ask you."

"Anything, what do you need?"

"I'd like to make arrangements for you to be Andy's guardian if something happens to me?"

"Nothing would please me more Andrew." Andrew looked at his watch, saying, "I've got an appointment, but I'll stop by on my way home."

"That's fine, Andrew," John said as he stood up and extended his hand to Andrew.

As Andrew held John's hand, he smiled and said, "Now I know why you have always looked familiar. I thought we had met before but could never remember where." Andrew smiled. "You sat next to me on the plane the day Harold and Sarah were killed."

"That's right, Andrew. I knew you would remember when the time was right."

· · · · · · · · · · · · · · · · · · · ·

Andrew stopped by the bank and spent a few minutes with Bob then kept his appointment with Don Realson, the lawyer Harold wrote about in his letter to Andy.

Don was a man in his early sixties but looked much younger. He greeted Andrew with a warm handshake and ushered him into his office. "Now fill me in, Andrew. What can I do for you?"

Andrew spent the next hour bringing Don up-to-date on everything that had happened since Harold and Sarah died. After a few minutes of reflecting, Don said, "This doesn't surprise me. Harold warned me that there would be repercussions when Margaret found out what he was worth. What do you want to do?"

Andrew took a deep breath and said, "I want you to draw up the necessary papers to transfer all of Andy's inheritance into a trust fund. In my mind, if Andy has twenty thousand a year plus his college and living expenses, that should be enough until he graduates. Will that be a problem?"

"No. I have a letter written in Harold's hand signed by both he and Sarah that states you will have final authority and irrevocable custody of Andy unless you decide differently."

"I'm glad you mentioned that because there is one more thing I want you to do for me. If anything should happen to me, I want Andy's affairs to be managed by John Staats. He is the youth pastor at Andy's church."

"You're sure you want me to draw that up?"

"Yes. Don, my interest is to protect Andy."

Don stood up and, taking Andrew's hand, said, "It will be as you wish, Andrew."

• • • • • • • • • • • • • • • • • • • •

Andrew drove by John's house. John was in the yard watering the flowers he had planted. He walked toward the car, and Andrew rolled down the window and shouted, "It's all taken care of, John." John gave Andrew thumbs-up and returned to his watering.

Andy was watching television when Andrew walked in the door. The phone rang, and when Andrew answered he heard Matt's voice. "Andrew, this is Matt. I just got home, and the housekeeper told me that Margaret was in jail. Do you know what's going on?"

"It would be better if you talked to Margaret, or at least come over and let's sit down. I think it's all a little complicated to discuss over the phone."

"Okay. I'm going down to the courthouse, but I'll stop on my way. I really want to get your side of this story before I see Margaret."

Thirty minutes later, Matt walked in the front door. Andy and Andrew were getting lunch ready. Andrew asked Matt if he had eaten. Matt said no, but he wasn't hungry. Matt sat down at the kitchen table and said, "Tell me what's going on, Andrew."

Andrew gave Matt his take on all that had happened. Matt just listened. When Andrew finished, Matt said, "None of this really surprises me. I'm ashamed to admit it, but I knew Margaret was up to something when she agreed to let the church kids have a party in our backyard. After all, you know what Margaret thinks about anything having to do with God."

Matt had a cup of coffee while Andrew and Andy ate lunch. "Well, I'd better get down to the courthouse." Matt said thank you and left. Andy and Andrew just looked at each other, realizing there was nothing to be said.

After lunch, Andrew said, "Let's go into the living room, son. There are some things we need to talk about." Andy knew by the tone of his papa's voice it was to be a serious discussion. They went to the living room and got settled in their favorite places.

Andrew started, "Andy, I know by now that you're aware your Aunt Margaret's actions have not been totally in your best interest. There have been a couple of things that she has done that you aren't aware of, nor should you concern yourself about them. However, the problems Maggie is facing now could be a turning point for her, or, being the bright lawyer I know her to be, she could walk away from it untouched. Either way, I know that at some point Margaret is going to try to control you and your inheritance. I want you to promise me that if anything should happen to me, you will get a hold of John as soon as possible. I've had papers drawn up that transfer your trust fund to John if anything happens to me before your twenty-first birthday. So call John before you talk to anyone, understand?"

"Sure. But why? You're all right, aren't you?"

Andrew chuckled and answered, "I'm fine, Andy. I just want to be sure you're okay."

"No problem, Papa."

Chapter Seventeen

When Matt got to the courthouse, Margaret and Dave were standing in the hall talking. Margaret looked up, and her eyes locked with Matt's for a brief second. Dave then had Margaret look at some papers, and after another brief conversation, Dave left by the side door. Margaret said as she approached Matt, "Let's get out of here." They left the courthouse in silence. The silence remained even after they were in the car. Matt started the car and quietly drove home.

After he put the car away, Matt was suddenly very hungry and started fixing himself a sandwich. Margaret leaned up against the counter, arms folded, and watched Matt. "Are you going to ask?"

"Would you tell me the truth if I did?"

Margaret's mouth was open, but she couldn't say anything. Matt had never taken a tone that held that level of accusation or harshness with her. Margaret found her voice but thought her next statement through very carefully before she spoke.

"Okay, Matt. I've made no secret of the fact that I think Dad is too old and too narrow-minded for Andy's good. I don't think he is capable of managing the amount of money Andy has, and he has much too much influence over Andy's mind. There, is that truth enough for you?"

"It doesn't explain why you were arrested, Margaret."

Again Margaret searched for just the right words. "First of all, I wasn't arrested. I was just held for questions. And second, I was questioned because a scared young girl that is in a lot of trouble found it easier to blame me than face the blame for her actions. Besides, from what I understand, it was a revenge thing from one of the kids on the baseball team at the school because Andy would not play for the team. Some kid named Dean Thompson gave Laura a package that was supposed to be your anniversary present to me, and she was to ask Andy to hold it for you until our anniversary."

"With your lawyer's mind, I'm surprised you can't see where that story just doesn't make sense. First of all, why would some kid named Dean Thompson have a gift for you from me? For that matter, how would a kid named Dean even know we were related to Andy? If I had bought you a gift and wanted Andy to hold it until our anniversary, which I wouldn't, I would have given it to Andy myself. And why would I ask this Dean kid to give it to Laura to give to Andy? Probably the most important, Dean Thompson died in an automobile accident last night."

That last bit of information hit Margaret like a ton of bricks. "Who told you that?"

"Your dad. I stopped by and had a talk with him this morning."

"How dare you? What gives you the right to discuss me with my dad or anyone?"

"Why would you assume our discussion was about you? However, you're right. And to answer your question, your actions gave me the right. You have been someone I don't know ever since Harold and Sarah died. Or should I say, ever since you found out our little nephew was a millionaire?"

Margaret was furious but knew she needed to be very careful how she responded to Matt's statement. She managed to softened her tone. "You're right, Matt. I have been under a lot of strain. I guess Harold's death hit me harder than I wanted to admit. Then with Dad moving in and taking over, well…it was all just too much."

Matt looked at Margaret like she was a total stranger. Margaret tried to match his stare but couldn't. She lowered her eyes and mumbled, "I need a hot shower."

The hot water felt refreshing but not cleansing as it peppered Margaret's body. Her thoughts were deep but scattered and unfocused. *What have I gotten myself into, Lord?* Realizing what she had just said startled her. That was as close as she had come to prayer in many years. The voice that had become very familiar stated, *No. You have almost accomplished what you set out to do. There is no evidence against you except for the word of a scared teenage girl who's so heavily implicated she would say anything to save her own neck. Let Laura take the fall. Dean is no longer a problem, and you can't be implicated.* Margaret finished her shower feeling resolved and once again sure of herself.

Chapter Eighteen

Andy had been deep in thought for most of the morning. "I need to talk to Laura, Papa."

"I understand why you would think that, but let me ask you a question. What could you say to Laura that would improve the situation? What words would turn around the harm she tried to do?"

"I can let her know that I forgive her and will stand beside her no matter what happens."

Andrew thought this through then answered, "You do what you need to do, son. You know I'll help any way I can."

Andy went to the phone and dialed Laura's number. Larry answered. "Hello, Larry? This is Andy. Is Laura there?"

"Yeah, she is, but I'm not sure she will come to the phone." The line was silent for several minutes.

"Hello, Andy."

"Hi, Laura. How are you holding up?"

"I've had better days." Andy could hear Laura's broken spirit.

"Laura, I needed you to know that I don't hold anything that happened against you. What you did was wrong, but I know there are other things at work here, and as a friend, I need you to know I understand. As a Christian, I need you to know that you are forgiven."

Again, the phone was silent. Andy said nothing more. It was hard to stay quiet, but he felt the next words needed to be Laura's.

Laura was openly sobbing. She managed, "Thank you, Andy. There is more to this story that you don't know. Can we talk face-to-face?"

"Any time, anywhere."

"Can I come over?"

"Sure. There is just me and Papa here; is that all right?"

"Yeah, I guess."

Within thirty minutes, Laura and Larry were at Andy's front door. Andrew answered the doorbell and told the kids that he and Andy were sitting in the kitchen. When Laura entered the kitchen and her eyes met Andy's for the first time since the party, Andy jumped up and wrapped his arms around Laura, praying that she would understand his support and Christian love. Laura buried her face in Andy's chest and wept. Andrew and Larry were unashamed as they watched two children of God embrace in love and forgiveness.

Andrew said, "Sit down, kids. Believe it or not, I actually made some chocolate chip cookies the other day, and they are edible." Andrew sat a plate of cookies, four glasses, and a pitcher of lemonade on the table. Andy was filling the glasses when the doorbell rang. Concern was felt more than seen by everyone. Andrew said, "Not to worry; I'll go."

John was standing at the door. "May I come in? I think you may need my help." Andrew was a bit confused by John's statement. He had been ready to turn whoever was at the door away. Instead, Andrew simply stepped back and allowed John to enter.

John went directly to the kitchen. He gently put his hand on Laura's shoulder and said, "Everything will be okay, Laura." Laura looked up with red-rimmed eyes but said nothing.

John sat down and said, "There is more to this, isn't there, Laura?" Laura looked surprised.

Andy said, "If you are around John very much, you'll get used to it. He knows. I don't know how, but he knows."

Laura confirmed John's statement by nodding her head. After a minute of reflective quiet, Laura began, "The reason I said there was dope in the package isn't the reason you think, Andy. A couple of days before the party, Dean called and asked me if he could meet me at the park because there was something very important he needed me to do for your aunt. He told me to be sure no one knew we were meeting. I met Dean, and before he said anything, he made me promise that I would never tell anyone what he was about to say." Laura stopped.

"He told me that he had gotten himself mixed up with this guy who sold drugs. He bought some a couple of times, and then the guy told him that if he sold a package, his next fix would be free. Dean got scared. He really didn't want to get mixed up in selling dope and wanted nothing more to do with that guy. He knew your aunt Margaret was a lawyer because I guess you had mentioned it at some point. He also knew my aunt worked for her, and that's why he got in touch with me. He asked me if I would ask Mrs. Selby if she could help. I called your aunt and told her the story. I was really kind of surprised, but she said she would be glad to help Andy's friend.

"Dean and I met the day before the party, and he gave me the package and said Mrs. Selby told him that I was to give it to you. Naturally, no one wanted you to know what was in it, so it was wrapped in wedding paper, and he made up the story about the anniversary gift. The real story was that Dean had the stuff when he met with Mrs. Selby. He said she didn't touch the box and didn't want to look inside. She explained that the seller's fingerprints would be on the package and that would help her make sure that Dean wasn't bothered again by the guy. She said that the package needed to be kept somewhere that no one would ever think of looking but somewhere she could get her hands on it when she needed it. Since you were her nephew, she could get to you any time she wanted, and no one would think anything of it. Dean didn't want you to know he was mixed up in anything, so the problem was how to get you to take a package that you wouldn't open."

Again, Laura paused then finished with, "That's where I came in. I thought I was hiding evidence for your aunt and you weren't really involved with any of it. Oh, Andy, I'm so sorry. Please forgive me?"

"I already have, Laura."

John and Andrew gave each other a knowing glance. John said, "We need to bring the Father into this." He began to pray. "Father, we know you knew all this before and as it was happening. We know you know the destructive forces that are behind all that's happened. What we don't know, Father, is what you want us to do. We need to be in your will in every step we take now. Please open our minds to your perfect plan. Give your children the peace that comes from your mercy and grace when we know our actions have been pleasing and in accordance to your Word. We stand before you with this request through and with the authority of Jesus Christ. Amen.

"Laura, did you tell this story to the police?"

"Yes, but Mrs. Selby came in later and told them it was a lie, so it was her word against mine. How can I stand against her? She's a lawyer, and after all, it wasn't her that had the package; it was me."

"Not to worry, Laura. Correcting this problem is already in the works."

"What do you mean, John?" Andrew asked.

"After Laura was arrested, I found Dean. I told him what had happened at the party, so he knew he had been implicated in the problem. I told him innocent people were about to pay a price for his mistake and asked him to go down to the police department with me to straighten things out. He said that it was probably the right thing to do and he would meet me there in a couple of hours. I was going to go down to headquarters anyway to see if there was something I could do for Laura, Larry, and their aunt. That's when I heard the news that Dean had been killed in a car accident."

Andrew said, "So either Dean was on his way to the police department and had a wreck, or he knew he would be found out and deliberately ran his car over the embankment." Everyone was thinking about a third alternative, given the type of people Dean had been mixed up with—foul play—but no one said it out loud.

John continued, "What we have to do now is find Laura a good Christian lawyer."

"That's not a problem. I just happen to know an excellent lawyer—Don Realson."

About an hour later, Laura and Larry said they had to go. John also said he was late for an appointment. Andrew and Andy walked them to the door. Andrew started toward the kitchen to clean up the table when Andy said, "We both know who is behind this, don't we, Papa?"

Tears welled up in Andrew's eyes as he turned toward Andy. "Yes, son. We do."

Andy followed Andrew back into the kitchen, but before they picked up the first glass, the room was filled with a sickening smell. Andrew immediately told Andy to pray. Before Andy could ask questions, the two men sat down and, joining hands, began to pray. "Lord, we rebuke the presence of evil in this house. We know the enemy of God is at work here and would like to destroy our resolve to be your servants. We ask in the name of Jesus Christ that you raise a hedge around us and this house and allow us to feel your safety and assurance that by your command only will evil be allowed near us. In Jesus's holy name. Amen."

Haphak had rushed into the kitchen with a horde of demons when Andrew and Andy had walked their guests to the door. He had been instructed to do everything in his power to plant doubt and fear and destroy any seeds of trust that may have been planted. He recoiled and turned away when Andrew mentioned the name above all names, but his determination and resolve remained. The fear he had planned for Andy turned inward as he became aware that there was another power present. He turned back toward Andy and saw Nahal, Darak, and Lachotaum standing between them. Their swords were raised and ready.

Andrew knew a great and very important battle was about to begin. He told Andy to continue to pray for protection, and he did the same. The two were suddenly aware of a change in the room and opened their eyes. The astonishment they felt was on the verge of overpowering them when they both heard, "Be not afraid, for I am with you." The room was divided in half, with Andrew, Andy, and three men in one half and what looked like a dozen men standing on the other side. The three men seemed to be taller than the ceiling but were not hampered by the structure's height. They were dressed in suits. One was white, one suit was blue, and one was green. The colors were vibrant. They had swords in their hands, and the swords looked like they were on fire, but there was no heat coming from the flame. They stood directly in front of Andrew and Andy.

The men on the other side of the room were dressed in dark clothing. They were cowering and confused. Nothing happened. Then Andrew looked in the center of the group on the other side of the room. Andy also looked, and they saw what they could only describe as a black hole appearing out of nowhere. Nahal, Darak and Lachotaum planted their feet as if ready for battle, but they were looking up. Andy and Andrew followed their gaze, and their bodies flooded with excitement as they saw hundreds of men in white with swords headed right for them. It was almost more than they could do not to try to move out of the way, but neither one could move. The men on the other side of the room also saw what was coming and looked to the black hole with anticipation and instruction. Arms seem to rise from the sides of the black hole, and the floor was alive as more and more darkly-dressed beings entered the room.

Andy heard his papa saying, "Cover us in your blood, Savior." Andy followed Andrew's lead of pleading the blood. The battle began. Both sides were suddenly armed with swords. Andrew and Andy saw that each time a being in dark was struck by a flaming sword, they faded into the floor with a yell of remorse that almost made one feel sorry for them. When a dark sword hit its mark on a being in white, he ascended, and ten more in white took his place.

Andy lost track of time; he thought it had to have been hours since Laura, Larry, and John left. Finally, they heard the sound of thunder from a voice that declared, "*Enough!*" Suddenly everything stopped and there was perfect silence. The voice from the black hole was also strong as they heard it declare, "This is not over."

Andrew and Andy were alone, or at least as far as they could see. They looked at the clock and realized that less than a minute had passed since they said good-bye to their guests at the front door. Neither one could say a word. Even if they could have found their voices, words were just simply not appropriate, except for the three from Andrew: "Thank you, Father."

The ringing phone broke the spell. Andy answered, "Hello!"

John's voice asked, "Are you two all right? I cancelled my appointment, came home, and have been in constant intercessory prayer since I left your house." When Andy was quiet for a long period of time, Andrew walked over and took the phone.

"Hello, John. This is Andrew. We are fine, and you have our thanks. We can talk later, but I'm sure you will not be astonished about what we saw."

"You are right, in a way, Andrew. But the works of the Almighty never cease to amaze me."

When Andrew hung up, Andy just stood there and stared at him. He said, "I'm not even going to ask how you knew it was John."

Andrew just smiled and walked out of the room. Andy soon realized that he was all alone in the kitchen. His first thought was to be a brave Christian warrior, but he soon realized that he felt a little anxious being there alone and decided to leave the room too.

Chapter Nineteen

Life almost returned to normal over the next several weeks. Andrew had retained Don Realson to defend Laura. The youth group had buzzed with rumors and talk for a while, but that too had been forgotten as they turned their attention to the daily routine of living. The summer had come and gone, and Andy's final year of high school began. Matt called Andrew in late October and said there had been an investigation into Dean's death. They had declared the event an accident. He also told Andrew that a hearing date had been set for the first week in November.

Andrew and Andy knew an investigation had been going on since the party, as policemen and detectives had been to the house many times. At one point, they had shown up with a search warrant. Don Realson just happened to be there, and even though a search had been conducted, it was completed in an orderly manner.

The day of the hearing finally arrived, and Andy was filled with apprehension. He wasn't sure if his feelings were about what would be revealed and the outcome or seeing Aunt Margaret. Andrew also felt apprehension about seeing Maggie. They had not talked or seen each other since the night of the party. The hearing was closed to everyone except the judge; Margaret and her lawyer, Dave; Laura and her lawyer, Don; Andy; Andrew; John; one policeman; and the detective who had been at the Selbys' the night of the party.

Before they began, Don said, "There might be one more person with important information, Your Honor, but I would like to reserve the name of that person until you determine if another witness is necessary." The judge rubbed his chin, thinking about Don's statement, then said, "Very well. Since this is an informal hearing, I'll allow it. Now let's get to the bottom of this. Don, since you have the floor, you begin."

Don told Laura's story exactly as she had explained it to everyone at the kitchen table. Several times during his speech, Margaret leaned over and whispered something to Dave. Finally it was Dave's turn.

He cleared his voice and began with, "There has been a misunderstanding about my client's involvement, Your Honor. Mrs. Selby was approached by Laura and asked to talk to Dean Thompson. As we all know, Mr. Thompson was killed in an accident and cannot be here to defend himself. However, it's true that Mr. Thompson told Mrs. Selby that he was in danger of being trapped by a drug pusher. He told her that he had evidence that would implicate this pusher and presented her with a box. The box was not open, nor did Mrs. Selby allow Dean to open the box. She told him that he needed to keep the box in a safe place, someplace where she would have access to the evidence when she needed it but did not want it in her possession at that time. Mrs. Selby will also admit that even though she had not seen the contents of the box, she had a pretty good idea what was in it. Dean told Mrs. Selby that he knew Andy was her nephew and that Andy and Laura had become good friends. He told her that when she needed the box, she should ask Andy—that he would have it. Laura had promised him that she would give it to Andy at the party that was held at the Selbys' the following night. Mrs. Selby regrets her implication in concealing evidence, but since no crime had been reported—indeed, she was not at that time certain of a crime—she felt like holding the evidence was in the best interest of her client."

When Dave finished, the judge looked at the detective and asked, "What light can you shed on this, Joe?"

Joe glanced at Margaret then added his story to those of Dave and Don. "On the night of May twenty-third, we received an anonymous tip that drugs would be present at a party at Mr. And Mrs. Selbys' home that evening and in the possession of Andy Staple. The person on the phone said he would be at the party but didn't want to get involved or become known, so when he saw the deal going down, he would buzz my cell phone and we could catch those involved. We waited in the car about half a block from the Selby home until we received the notice. We were told that we should ask to see Andy Staple and he would have the drugs in his possession.

"When we got to the party, we took Andy into the house to question and search him. Andy did not have the drugs in his possession. Another policeman searched the kids outside. The girl Andy was with, Laura, had a package wrapped in wedding paper in her pocket. Laura was taken to police headquarters for further questioning. Since Andy did not have the drugs and Laura indicated that he had no knowledge of the package or what was going on, we told Andy to go home but we would certainly be talking to him very soon.

"During questioning, Laura told us the same story her lawyer has told you here today. We have searched the Staple' home for any additional evidence that would implicate Andy and found nothing. We've also talked with Andy's friends, teachers, and associates and have found no reason to believe that he was involved in any way, Your Honor."

John was next and told the judge the conversation he had with Dean the night of his death. The judge called a three-hour recess, stating that he would consider what he heard and they should all return to his chambers at three that same afternoon.

Andrew asked John to join him and Andy for lunch, and John accepted. There had been many discussions about what happened in the kitchen the day they had all met. As Andrew had predicted, John was in awe of the control God takes in the defense of his children but was not surprised. Andy had shared that for some reason he was now aware of people in a totally different way. When pressed, he said, "It's really hard to explain. It's like I don't really see the person anymore; I see their spirit. Oh, I don't mean I actually see their spiritual body, but I'm not really aware or care about what they are wearing or if they are pretty, ugly, black, or white. I also feel love and concern for people. It's kind of weird. Even strangers…I seem to sense if they need prayer and find my spirit praying for them. I am also aware of a person's intentions. Don't ask me to really explain this one, but somehow I know if a person is truthful or means someone else harm. I saw this problem surrounding both Aunt Margaret, Dave, and, surprisingly, the policeman that testified this morning."

Andrew and John shared a look and a smile. Andy caught the exchange and asked, "Okay, you two, let me in on the joke."

"It's no joke, Andy; it's the Holy Spirit beginning his work in your life. He is preparing and teaching you one step at a time for the work God has for you to do," John offered.

All Andy could say was "Wow!" They all shared a chuckle and went into Wendy's for a hamburger.

● ● ● ● ● ● ● ● ● ● ● ● ● ● ● ● ●

Dave and Margaret also went to lunch but went to a restaurant in a nearby town to be reasonably sure they would not run into anyone at the hearing. When their food had been served, Dave said, "I know you know how important it is to make sure your defense knows everything there is about a case, Margaret. Is there anything I don't know?"

Margaret didn't answer right away. She knew what Dave was asking, but she thought that as far as this case went, he knew everything he needed to know. Her motives behind some of the plans she held for Andy and his future were not important in this hearing, and she had to admit that if he had known some of her reasons, it would not help. She looked Dave straight in the eye and said, "Dave, you know all there is to know about this case."

At three that afternoon, they were all sitting in the judge's chambers, waiting for his entrance. At five minutes after the hour, Judge Bacon walked in, set his papers down on his desk, and sat down. He opened a file, looked up, and said, "We have a unique situation here. As I see it, we have a young man that found himself in harm's way and asked for legal counsel to prevent himself from getting in over his head with drug dealers. We have a lawyer that states her actions were only to protect her client and to this end acted in his best interest. We have a young woman who thought she was helping everyone, not realizing that she was, in fact, breaking the law by not reporting the possession of drugs. It is in her favor, though, that she was told her actions were known and had been sanctioned by legal counsel." Judge Bacon gave Margaret a look of disgust as he made this statement. "It is also in her favor that her fingerprints were not found on the envelope containing the narcotic. One thing that helps everyone here today is the fact that there was only one set of prints on the wrapped package—those belonging to Dean Thompson. Andy was implicated simply by the fact that he knew and was known by all the players. And we have a concerned citizen who tried to intervene and lead the young boy, Dean, to do the right thing."

Pausing for a second, he continued, "There are some things in this case that are fuzzy, to say the least. However, since the only person who could clarify these uncertainties is dead, I fear there is no way we will ever know the truth. I am releasing all of you. There is a lack of evidence to charge or hold anyone."

His tone became very firm, and looking directly at Margaret, he said, "Know this: the investigation into this is far from over. I am ordering that every story recorded here today be gone over with a fine-tooth comb, every word checked and double-checked, and if I find that anyone has added or left out one fact, I promise we will once again meet, and this time, it will be in the courtroom." With that, Judge Bacon stood up, picked up his folder, and left the room.

When the door closed behind the judge, Margaret saw Dave looking at her with a concern that made her feel uneasy. In rather a gleeful sound that was much too cheerful for the occasion, Margaret stood up and said, "That went rather well, don't you think?"

Everyone in the room just stared at her. She felt her face growing warm, and she picked up her briefcase and left the room. Everyone else filed out of the room in complete silence. When they reached the parking lot, Laura gave John a hug, then Andrew, and said, "I know you've both been praying for me." She reached out and shook Don's hand. "I don't even have the words I need to say to you, Mr. Realson."

"It's Don, Laura, and there is no need to say anything. More was accomplished here today than you know."

As Don turned to walk to his car, he heard a now-familiar voice. "Counselor, may I speak with you?" He turned to see Margaret headed in his direction.

"What can I do for you, Mrs. Selby?"

"You did a great job in there for Laura, and I wanted to thank you. You, of course, know that she is a good friend of my nephew, Andy."

"Yes, Andy, his grandfather, and I have had many interesting conversations."

Margaret wasn't sure she liked the implication behind what Don had just said. She continued cautiously with, "There are some legal concerns about Andy and his future that I would like to discuss with you, Mr. Realson. Since Andy is my nephew, I feel there would be a conflict of interest perceived if my law firm examined my findings."

Don Realson did not answer right away. He decided to wait until it was apparent that Mrs. Selby was uncomfortable with the silence. When fully satisfied that Margaret was on the verge of squirming, he said, "I'm afraid that isn't possible, Mrs. Selby. You see, I represent Andrew and Andy in the matter of Andy's future, and I must tell you, off the record, of course, that at this point you are not part of that future in any way, shape, or form." With that and a crisp, "Good day," Don walked to his car, leaving Margaret standing alone and confused.

Margaret had a debriefing session with Dave scheduled at their office. When she walked into Dave's office, she was stunned to find all the partners there waiting for her. Without a word, she walked to her usual chair and sat down. Dave, being one of the senior partners, began speaking as he tapped the eraser end of his pencil on the table. "Margaret, we have documents that tell us you have put your future above the expectations and goals of this company. You are a good lawyer, Margaret, but your involvement in this, beyond that of legal counsel, has put us all in a position we do not want. It has been decided that until this investigation is completely over and closed, you will be on leave. Since it is Friday afternoon, you will be asked to clean out your desk and leave the building. You will of course receive six months of full pay, and if you have not been allowed to return at the end of six months, you will be terminated from any further association with this firm."

Margaret was stunned. Her mind flooded with legal ramifications for their actions, lines in her defense, and what documents they were speaking about, but she could say nothing. Instead, she simply stood up and walked out of the room. When her desk was emptied, she drove home. All she could think of was having Matt hold her and tell her that everything would be all right. She glanced at her watch and wondered if he had remembered that it was his night to stop and buy takeout for their dinner. When she pulled into the driveway and he wasn't home yet, she let out a sigh of relief. The last thing she wanted to do was cook.

Margaret let herself into the side door and turned off the alarm. Walking into the kitchen to see if there was something cold to drink, Margaret saw a note on the refrigerator.

Margaret, the day we married, I promised to love the woman I married forever.

Margaret smiled and continued reading.

However, you are not the woman I married. You have become a person I find it difficult to respect or believe. There are some things I must work out within myself, Margaret, without you. I hope and, yes, even pray that you will do the same.

Always,

Matt

Margaret stood in front of the refrigerator and stared at the note as her eyes filled with tears and her heart broke. She walked to the table and sat down. Margaret had grown accustomed to listening to her thoughts rather than forming them. She listened to herself say, *How dare he do this to me. I've never been unfaithful, even though there have been many times I could have. And what about this Don Realson thing? If he thinks he can rule me out of Andy's life, he has another think coming.* She felt her mind targeting her father and flooding with revengeful, vile impressions toward him. Margaret's head shot up, and she screamed, "My God! These are not my thoughts. Matt is right; I am not doing my own thinking or being myself."

Maggie's mind saw her mother bustling around in the old farm kitchen, humming a chorus from church or just praying in music. She remembered how much her dad meant to her while she was growing up and how supportive they all were for each other when Nan died. What was it that had caused so much bitterness toward God and ultimately everyone who looked to Him for peace and support? Her face became wet with tears as the realization hit her that she was the person responsible for all her anger and pain. God had been fighting for her and made it clear that until the final minute He would not give her up easily. She had turned her back on Him, but He had never forsaken or left her. Dad was right; she had started in the spirit and then decided she could handle whatever happened with her intellect, training, and money. She felt sick; her chest hurt so badly she thought she might be having a heart attack. Finally, Margaret heard herself say, "God, forgive me. Help me. You are the only one I have left. You have every right to forsake me as I have forsaken you, and if that is what you decide, I will understand. But I will put a stop to this madness right now. If you will once again allow me to know that I have a chance to be a member of your family, I will never do anything that will harm or stop Andy from becoming all you want him to become."

Margaret opened her eyes, and for the first time in a long time, she felt clean. She was far from happy, but there was a sense of satisfaction about herself that she didn't know she missed until this moment. The doorbell broke her thought. She thought about not answering it but found she was on her way to the door even as she thought the way the old Margaret would have—putting Margaret first. She opened the door, and there stood Andrew with arms stretched out ready to hold her. She rushed into his arms and sobbed for forgiveness. They went back into the kitchen and sat down.

Andrew began, "Maggie, Don told me about your conversation, and I think it's only fair to explain to you what's happened." Andrew waited for Margaret to respond. She looked at her dad with a look that told Andrew she had changed.

"Dad, I will support whatever you decide for Andy. I need to confess that had you said anything contrary to my plans for Andy yesterday, I was prepared to fight you. Just so you know, I was fired today. They called it a leave of absence, but I was fired. Also, here, read this." She pushed the note from Matt toward Andrew.

Andrew read the note and put his hand over Maggie's when he finished. "Maggie, everything is going to be fine. It will take some time to undo what's been done, but trust me, it will work out for the best."

Margaret's mind remembered something she had heard her mother say, something about everything working out for the good of those who love God. She knew there had to be very few people who loved God more than Andrew and Andy, so she smiled with the knowledge of truth.

Andrew explained that Harold had made provisions in a document he filed and left with Don Realson. "If for some reason I was unable to be Andy's guardian, I would have the power to name the person who would take my place. If I died suddenly, then Don Realson was appointed to make the decision about Andy's guardianship. You see, Margaret, there never was an opening for you to control Andy or his money." Andrew knew he had been blunt with this last statement, but it was a time for hard truth so the air could be cleared once and for all.

Margaret smiled at her dad and answered, "It's okay, Dad. Guess there were some things I needed to learn, and the most important was that even though I had given up on God, he hadn't given up on me."

"Never."

"When I feel like I'm walking on solid ground again, there are some things that have been happening to me that I must talk to you or someone about…feelings and thoughts that should have scared me to death, now that I look back at them."

"I can help you understand, but the greatest news I have now is that you won't be alone or have to put up with it any longer. Just remember that I'm always here for you, anytime, day or night, and will continue to lift you up in prayer."

It had been years since Margaret and Andrew had been able to just talk as father and daughter, but for the next couple of hours, that's exactly what they did. Andrew went home with a light heart full of thanks.

* * * * * * * * * * * * * * * * * *

Epilogue

Two birthdays had come and gone for Andy since the death of his parents. He and Laura ran into each other and remained good friends but were no longer dating. He had finally made the decision to go to Columbia Bible College on the outskirts of Portland. He and Andrew had discussed the future with Margaret, and everyone agreed the best thing to do was to either lease or sell the house in Pasco, whichever came first. Andrew would move back to the farm and get it ready to sell also, as he was getting too old to keep it up. The couple of years he had been away from the farm allowed him to realize how much work it had been.

Margaret was reinstated with the Tory and Banson law firm, and the atmosphere was strained for a short period, but they all settled into a familiar routine as business picked up. She still had feelings of guilt when she thought about how much damage she could have caused if things had gone her way. Matt called about once a week, but he wasn't ready to return home yet. He was shocked when Margaret told him she understood and that whenever he did decide, she would be waiting.

John told Andrew that he would also be moving to the Portland area. He had been offered the senior pastor's position at the Baptist church in Pasco but had turned it down. His duty was to be available when Andy was ready for the next step.

It would be sooner than anyone thought.

For Further Study

The following scriptures are those found in the story and many I used to present my purpose for adding situations that occurred. I pray that you will never find yourself in any of these predicaments, but if you do, you will know that there is a scripture that will help you through them.

Chapter One

Proverbs 22:6: "Train up a child in the way he should go, and when he is old he will not turn from it."

Ephesians 6:4: "Fathers, do not exasperate your children, instead, bring them up in the training and instruction of the Lord."

Chapter Two

Job 36:18–19: "Be careful that no one entices you by riches; do not let a large bribe turn you aside. Would your wealth or even all your mighty efforts sustain you so you would not be in distress?"

Psalm 31:14: "But I am trusting you, O Lord, saying, 'You are my God!'"

Psalm 52:8–9: "But I am like an olive tree, thriving in the house of God. I trust in God's unfailing love forever and ever. I will praise you forever, O God, for what you have done."

Psalm 143:8: "Let me hear of your unfailing love to me in the morning, for I am trusting you. Show me where to walk, for I have come to you in prayer."

Psalm 38:15: "I wait for you, O Lord; you will answer, O Lord my God."

James 4:7: "Submit yourselves, then, to God. Resist the devil, and he will flee from you."

Psalm 103:9–12: "He will not always accuse, nor will he harbor his anger forever; he does not treat us as our sins deserve or repay us according to our iniquities. For as high as the heavens are above the earth, so great is his love for those who fear him; as far as the east is from the west, so far has he removed our transgressions from us."

Psalm 9:10: "Those who know your name will trust in you, for you, Lord, have never forsaken those who seek you."

Proverbs 8:17: "I love those who love me, and those who seek me find me."

Proverbs 2:5–6: "Then you will understand the fear of the Lord and find the knowledge of God. For the Lord gives wisdom, and from his mouth come knowledge and understanding."

Hebrews 13:2: "Do not forget to entertain strangers, for by so doing some people have entertained angels without knowing it."

Chapter Three

Psalm 2:1: "Serve the Lord with fear and rejoice with trembling."

Psalm 85:9–13: "Surely his salvation is near those who fear him, that his glory may dwell in our land."

2 Corinthians 5:7: "We live by faith, not by sight."

Matthew 7:13–14: "Enter through the narrow gate. For wide is the gate and broad is the road that leads to destruction, and many enter through it. But small is the gate and narrow the road that leads to life, and only a few find it."

Revelation 4:5: "From the throne came flashes of lightning, rumblings and peals of thunder. Before the throne, seven lamps were blazing. These are the seven spirits of God."

1 Corinthians 13:12: "Now we see but a poor reflection as in a mirror; then we shall see face to face. Now I know in part; then I shall know fully, even as I am fully known."

Ephesians 6:12: "For our struggle is not against flesh and blood, but against the rulers, against the authorities, against the powers of this dark world and against the spiritual forces of evil in the heavenly realms."

1 Peter 5:8: "Be self-controlled and alert. Your enemy the devil prowls around like a roaring lion looking for someone to devour."

1 Corinthians 10:13: "No temptation has seized you except what is common to man. And God is faithful; he will not let you be tempted beyond what you can bear. But when you are tempted, he will also provide a way out so that you can stand up under it."

Psalm 31:5: "I entrust my spirit into your hand. Rescue me, Lord, for you are a faithful God."

Matthew 7:13–14: "Enter through the narrow gate. For wide is the gate and broad is the road that leads to destruction, and many enter through it. But small is the gate and narrow the road that leads to life, and only a few find it."

Proverbs 25:16: "If you find honey, eat just enough—too much of it, and you will vomit."

Revelation 21:8: "But the cowardly, the unbelieving, the vile, the murderers, the sexually immoral, those who practice magic arts, the idolaters and all liars—their place will be in the fiery lake of burning sulfur. This is the second death."

Luke 4:5–6: "The devil led him up to a high place and showed him in an instant all the kingdoms of the world. And he said to him, 'I will give you all their authority and splendor, for it has been given to me, and I can give it to anyone I want to.'"

Chapter Four

Psalm 38:8: "I am feeble and utterly crushed; I groan in anguish of heart."

Psalm 25:16–17: "Turn to me and be gracious to me, for I am lonely and afflicted. The troubles of my heart have multiplied; free me from my anguish."

Luke 8:30–31: "Jesus asked him, 'What is your name?' 'Legion,' he replied, because many demons had gone into him. And they begged him repeatedly not to order them to go into the Abyss."

1 Corinthians 1:27: "But God chose the foolish things of the world to shame the wise; God chose the weak things of the world to shame the strong."

Chapter Five

Deuteronomy 20:4: "For the LORD your God is the one who goes with you to fight for you against your enemies to give you victory."

Psalm 44:6–7: "I do not trust in my bow, my sword does not bring me victory; but you give us victory over our enemies, you put our adversaries to shame."

Proverbs 2:7–8: "He holds victory in store for the upright; he is a shield to those whose walk is blameless, for he guards the course of the just and protects the way of his faithful ones."

Deuteronomy 8:3: "He humbled you, causing you to hunger and then feeding you with manna, which neither you nor your fathers had known, to teach you that man does not live on bread alone but on every word that comes from the mouth of the LORD."

Matthew 4:4: "Jesus answered, 'It is written: "Man does not live on bread alone, but on every word that comes from the mouth of God."'"

Exodus 14:14: "The LORD himself will fight for you. You won't have to lift a finger in your defense!"

Ephesians 6:15: "...and with your feet fitted with the readiness that comes from the gospel of peace."

Chapter Six

Galatians 4:6: "Because you are sons, God sent the Spirit of his Son into our hearts, the Spirit who calls out, 'Abba, Father.'"

John 4:23–24: "Yet a time is coming and has now come when the true worshipers will worship the Father in spirit and truth, for they are the kind of worshipers the Father seeks. God is spirit, and his worshipers must worship in spirit and in truth."

Proverbs 20:12: "Ears to hear and eyes to see—both are gifts from the LORD."

Psalm 10:14: "But you, O God, do see trouble and grief; you consider it to take it in hand. The victim commits himself to you; you are the helper of the fatherless."

2 Corinthians 5:6: "Therefore we are always confident and know that as long as we are at home in the body we are away from the Lord."

Chapter Seven

1 Corinthians 15:54–57: "When the perishable has been clothed with the imperishable, and the mortal with immortality, then the saying that is written will come true: 'Death has been swallowed up in victory. Where, O death, is your victory? Where, O death, is your sting? The sting of death is sin, and the power of sin is the law. But thanks be to God! He gives us the victory through our Lord Jesus Christ.'"

1 Timothy 6:17–19: "Command those who are rich in this present world not to be arrogant nor to put their hope in wealth, which is so

uncertain, but to put their hope in God, who richly provides us with everything for our enjoyment. Command them to do good, to be rich in good deeds, and to be generous and willing to share. In this way they will lay up treasure for themselves as a firm foundation for the coming age, so that they may take hold of the life that is truly life."

Ephesians 1:17–18: "I keep asking that the God of our Lord Jesus Christ, the glorious Father, may give you the Spirit of wisdom and revelation, so that you may know him better. I pray also that the eyes of your heart may be enlightened in order that you may know the hope to which he has called you, the riches of his glorious inheritance in the saints."

1 Samuel 2:7–8: "The Lord sends poverty and wealth; he humbles and he exalts. He raises the poor from the dust and lifts the needy from the ash heap; he seats them with princes and has them inherit a throne of honor. For the foundations of the earth are the Lord's; upon them he has set the world."

Psalm 39:6–7: "Man is a mere phantom as he goes to and fro: He bustles about, but only in vain; he heaps up wealth, not knowing who will get it. But now, Lord, what do I look for? My hope is in you."

Proverbs 8:18–21: "With me are riches and honor, enduring wealth and prosperity. My fruit is better than fine gold; what I yield surpasses choice silver. I walk in the way of righteousness, along the paths of justice, bestowing wealth on those who love me and making their treasuries full."

Matthew 6:19–21: "Do not store up for yourselves treasures on earth, where moth and rust destroy, and where thieves break in and steal. But store up for yourselves treasures in heaven, where moth and rust do not destroy, and where thieves do not break in and steal. For where your treasure is, there your heart will be also."

Luke 12:33–34: "Sell your possessions and give to the poor. Provide purses for yourselves that will not wear out, a treasure in heaven that will not be exhausted, where no thief comes near and no moth destroys. For where your treasure is, there your heart will be also."

Psalm 73:3–12: "For I envied the arrogant when I saw the prosperity of the wicked. They have no struggles; their bodies are healthy and strong. They are free from the burdens common to man; they are not plagued by human ills. Therefore pride is their necklace; they clothe themselves with violence. From their callous hearts comes iniquity; the evil conceits of their minds know no limits. They scoff, and speak with malice; in their arrogance they threaten oppression. Their mouths lay claim to heaven, and their tongues take possession of the earth. Therefore their people turn to them and drink up waters in abundance. They say, "How can God know? Does the Most High have knowledge?"

Chapter Eight

Deuteronomy 13:6–8: "If your very own brother, or your son or daughter, or the wife you love, or your closest friend secretly entices you, saying, 'Let us go and worship other gods' (gods that neither you nor your fathers have known, gods of the peoples around you, whether near or far, from one end of the land to the other), do not yield to him or listen to him. Show him no pity. Do not spare him or shield him."

Proverbs 18:24: "A man of many companions may come to ruin, but there is a friend who sticks closer than a brother."

Proverbs 10:4: "Lazy hands make a man poor, but diligent hands bring wealth."

Proverbs 10:22: "The blessing of the LORD brings wealth, and he adds no trouble to it."

Proverbs 11:28: "Whoever trusts in his riches will fall, but the righteous will thrive like a green leaf."

Proverbs 13:7: "One man pretends to be rich, yet has nothing; another pretends to be poor, yet has great wealth."

Proverbs 15:6: "The house of the righteous contains great treasure, but the income of the wicked brings them trouble."

Proverbs 28:20: "A faithful man will be richly blessed, but one eager to get rich will not go unpunished."

Ecclesiastes 5:10: "Whoever loves money never has money enough; whoever loves wealth is never satisfied with his income. This too is meaningless."

Deuteronomy 32:36–37: "Indeed, the LORD will judge his people, and he will change his mind about his servants, when he sees their strength is gone and no one is left, slave or free. Then he will ask, 'Where are their gods, the rocks they fled to for refuge?'"

Proverbs 1:23–33: "If you had responded to my rebuke, I would have poured out my heart to you and made my thoughts known to you. But since you rejected me when I called and no one gave heed when I stretched out my hand, since you ignored all my advice and would not accept my rebuke, I in turn will laugh at your disaster; I will mock when calamity overtakes you—when calamity overtakes you like a storm, when disaster sweeps over you like a whirlwind, when distress and trouble overwhelm you. Then they will call to me but I will not answer; they will look for me but will not find me. Since they hated knowledge and did not choose to fear the LORD, since they would not accept my advice and spurned my rebuke, they will eat the fruit of their ways and be filled with the fruit of their schemes. For the waywardness of the simple will kill them, and the complacency of fools will destroy them; but whoever listens to me will live in safety and be at ease, without fear of harm."

Lamentations 3:32–33: "Though he brings grief, he also shows compassion according to the greatness of his unfailing love. For he does not enjoy hurting people or causing them sorrow."

Psalm 88:8–9: "You have taken from me my closest friends and have made me repulsive to them. I am confined and cannot escape; my eyes are dim with grief. I call to you, O LORD, every day; I spread out my hands to you."

Chapter Nine

Job 1:10: "Have you not put a hedge around him and his household and everything he has? You have blessed the work of his hands, so that his flocks and herds are spread throughout the land."

Matthew 23:5–7: "Everything they do is done for men to see: They make their phylacteries wide and the tassels on their garments long; they love the place of honor at banquets and the most important seats in the synagogues; they love to be greeted in the marketplaces and to have men call them 'Rabbi.'"

Chapter Ten

Revelation 3:16: "So, because you are lukewarm—neither hot nor cold—I am about to spit you out of my mouth."

Exodus 31:3–5: "I have filled him with the Spirit of God, giving him great wisdom, intelligence, and skill in all kinds of crafts. He is able to create beautiful objects from gold, silver, and bronze. He is skilled in cutting and setting gemstones and in carving wood. Yes, he is a master at every craft!"

John 6:35–36: "Then Jesus declared, 'I am the bread of life. He who comes to me will never go hungry, and he who believes in me will never be thirsty. But as I told you, you have seen me and still you do not believe.'"

Chapter Eleven

Matthew 10:29–30: "Are not two sparrows sold for a penny? Yet not one of them will fall to the ground apart from the will of your Father. And even the very hairs of your head are all numbered."

Ecclesiastes 7:11–12: "Wisdom, like an inheritance, is a good thing and benefits those who see the sun. Wisdom is a shelter as money is a shelter, but the advantage of knowledge is this: that wisdom preserves the life of its possessor."

Mark 4:18–19: "Still others, like seed sown among thorns, hear the word; but the worries of this life, the deceitfulness of wealth and the desires for other things come in and choke the word, making it unfruitful."

1 Timothy 6:17–19: "Command those who are rich in this present world not to be arrogant nor to put their hope in wealth, which is so uncertain, but to put their hope in God, who richly provides us with everything for our enjoyment. Command them to do good, to be rich in good deeds, and to be generous and willing to share. In this way they will lay up treasure for themselves as a firm foundation for the coming age, so that they may take hold of the life that is truly life."

Chapter Twelve

Proverbs 3:5–6: "Trust in the LORD with all your heart; do not depend on your own understanding. Seek his will in all you do, and he will direct your paths."

Chapter Fifteen

Matthew 18:19–20: "I also tell you this: If two of you agree down here on earth concerning anything you ask, my Father in heaven will do it for you. For where two or three gather together because they are mine, I am there among them."